WEEKLY READER CHILDREN'S BOOK CLUB PRESENTS

MARGARET AND GEORGE OGAN

NUMBER ONE SON

FUNK & WAGNALLS   NEW YORK

ILLUSTRATED BY VIC DONAHUE

To Ray

Other books by the same authors

For Younger Readers

CHOICY

GOOFY FOOT

THE GREEN GALLOPER

For Teen-Age Readers

BACKYARD WINNER

DEVIL DRIVERS

PANCAKE SPECIAL

A PLACE FOR INGRID

Contents

⚓

NUMBER ONE SON

CHAPTER 1

~~~~~~~~~~~~~~~~~~~~~~~~~~

I Meet Tishi

⚓

One morning during last May, everything happened to
me. I don't hate school, even after so many years of it. Dad
could only finish sixth grade before he had to go to work.
"There's no such thing as too much education these days,"
he keeps telling me. "Get all you can, Paddy. There's no
excuse for ignorance any more."

Marina Junior High School on Fillmore Street, where
I'm a sophomore, is another reason I'm no dropout. It's a
four-story red-brick building with paved yards—just like
most of the other San Francisco city junior highs, but our
school spirit at Marina is terrific. The teachers are the
main reason for that because they get out and back every
school activity. They put in a lot more hours around school
than they get paid for, I guess.

That Monday morning in May it shouldn't have been
such a chore for me to get to school on time. I'm usually
punctual. Dad says it takes as much effort to be late as it

does to be on time. That could be. All I know is that I was
feeling fine, though my energy was missing. I did sleep
through the alarm clock, but that isn't unusual for me
lately. Mom claims it's because I'm growing so fast.

Big Dan Costello, Dad's father, who lives with us in
our house on Bay Street, told me once, "Off the record,
your father wasn't easy to roust out in the morning."

I can always depend on Big Dan to roust me out when
I don't hear the alarm. He was captain on the San Francisco police force until he retired eleven years ago. It was
the other members of the force who gave him the nick-
name of Big Dan. You can always depend on Big Dan for
things like getting you up in the morning.

"Rise and shine!" he booms at me. And he always stays
long enough to make sure I don't try to crawl back under
the covers.

Mom was up in Redwood City visiting our Aunt Mar-
ion who'd been sick, so my sister Megan was pinch-hitting
for her. "Don't be late to school, Pat," Megan said to me
when she pushed me out of the front door after breakfast.
"Here, don't forget your lunch."

"Thanks, and don't you be late, either."

Megan is in Nurses' Training at the University of California Medical Center on Parnassus Street near Golden
Gate Park. She has it rough when Mom's gone, because
Dad is a fisherman, and that means he starts the day at
four-thirty in the morning. That Monday my brother
Jerry, who is twenty-one, was fishing with Dad, so Megan
had to get their breakfast, and pack their lunches, too. But
Megan doesn't seem to mind. She's eighteen, which is
something Big Dan says she'll survive, but he isn't too sure

about the rest of us. When Megan takes over for Mom, though, it's a big deal with her.

"Did you brush your teeth?" she called, just as I reached the front gate. Mom always asks that question.

"I sure did, Big Sister."

It was one of those San Francisco May mornings when clouds of pure white fog push into the harbor through the Golden Gate and past the Presidio. It's bright and clear on the peninsula, though, and the water in the harbor is steel blue. You can hear the low, mellow tone of foghorns and the musical clang of bell buoys. The air is so fresh you can taste it. On this kind of morning, who likes to hurry?

It's only eight blocks from our house to school. I can make the distance in seven minutes, or sometimes five if I run a little. That morning, though, I couldn't shift up out of low gear, and the last bell rang just as I walked up the school steps.

Being lazy isn't a valid excuse for being late to school. Mrs. Fremont is the woman in the front office who makes out tardy slips. She's hard to convince with a phony excuse, so I didn't try.

"Well, Pat, what wonderful yarn do you have this morning?" she said when I came up to the office counter. "I should warn you that I've heard some good ones so far. None very original, however."

"I don't have any yarn made up," I told her. "I started in time, but I couldn't make myself walk fast enough."

She raised her eyebrows. "That is original." She reached for an unexcused tardy slip. "I'm afraid, though, that honesty is going to have to be its own reward."

Morning classes were bad. I booted an easy history question—something I knew—and, by misplacing the decimal points, I got seven wrong answers on an eight-question math quiz.

My day fell apart even more at lunch. I went through the cafeteria line for some milk and dessert. Looking for a table, I bumped a girl with my tray. It was really her fault, because she was too busy talking to her girl friend to see me coming, but I stopped and said, "I'm sorry."

At that moment a guy behind bumped me. My apple pie with ice cream and my milk went flying.

I mopped up the mess, while all the kids were making their usual bright remarks: "Do you have ten thumbs, Pat?" "Do it again, Pat—Joe didn't see you" "Give us an encore!" And I'd have to make do with only Megan's sandwiches and water!

A Megan sandwich is hard enough to eat even when you have plenty of milk. She likes olives and nuts chopped up and mixed with mayonnaise, spread on rye bread that's stale enough to be chewy, covered over with limp lettuce, and garnished with a dill pickle. Since Megan likes this mess, she thinks everyone does, and it's no use trying to convince her otherwise. It's healthy, she says.

Anyway, I started afternoon classes—healthy maybe, but hungry for sure. I was scheduled to make an oral book report in English, my first class after lunch. I had a sheaf of notes to talk from, but they were home on my dresser. I didn't discover that, though, until I was called on.

Ears burning, and wondering if I could get by, I stood up to recite without notes. Even though school was almost over for the summer, there was a new Japanese kid in the front row. According to the roll, his name was Ken Naka-mura.

Ken had jet black hair that was crewcut. His black eyes fixed on my face and stayed there, while he grinned expectantly. All those nice, even, white teeth confused me. What was so funny?

"My book is . . . was . . . *San Francisco Pageant*. It's written by a guy . . . by an *author* . . . whose name is Caldwell Charles Dobie." I paused because something about that name didn't sound right. "Dobie Caldwell Charles?" I said.

My English teacher, Mr. Morris, had started to scowl. Ken's hand popped up, his grin getting wider. "It's *Charles Caldwell Dobie*," he said, before Mr. Morris could call on him. "I read that book last term."

This joker was going to be a *big* help! I tried ignoring him, and went on, "It isn't exactly a history book, or anything like that. It does tell a lot about San Francisco's history, though."

"Pat?" Mr. Morris interrupted.

"Yes, sir?"

"Is this book, or is it not, a history?"

Ken's hand went up. "Mr. Dobie explains that he hasn't written an *exhaustive* history. San Francisco has too much history for anyone to be able to cram it all into one book, Mr. Dobie says in the preface. He says . . ."

The class was in stitches by this time. And now Megan's sandwich and my stomach began their own private war. Mr. Morris was rapping his desk with his knuckles, trying to stop the giggling. "Thank you, Mr. Nakamura," he said to Ken sarcastically, "but shall we let Pat bumble along in his own particular way?" He then asked me, "Hadn't you better use your notes? You're not doing too well without them."

"I *have* notes."

Mr. Morris gave me a pained smile. "Shall we refer to them, then?"

"I can't."

"Why not?"

"They're at home."

The class roared. Ken looked around, and then laughed with them.

"In a safe place, I hope?" Mr. Morris said, after he had quieted the class. He heaved a disgusted sigh. "Do the best you can, Pat. This is a captive audience, so they can't walk out on you. Go ahead."

I wished they'd all walk out and fall down the stairs— on top of Ken Nakamura! My best wasn't very good after that start. Mr. Morris gave me a D+. He then asked for class comment.

"Pat didn't mention the most interesting chapter in the book," Ken said brightly. "That's the one all about the San Francisco earthquake. The author tells about it exactly as he saw it."

It was time to put this new kid down, if I could. "That chapter wasn't very interesting to me," I said, "because my grandfather, Big Dan Costello, was there, too, as a police-man. He can really yarn about it."

Mr. Morris was suddenly interested. "Is your grandfa-ther still alive, Pat?"

"He sure is!"

"Do you suppose he could talk with the class one afternoon?"

"Yes, I guess so."

"Will you ask him? Anyone who was here in 1906 should have a great deal to tell us."

"I'll ask him."

I wished that I'd bitten my tongue instead. It was just three years ago that some ladies from an historical society tried to get Big Dan to lecture. Mom scolded him about the way he talked to them.

"All right, Kate, so I wasn't polite," he growled. "I'm not going to make a fool out of myself before a bunch of old hens."

I didn't like to think what Big Dan was going to say to me when I asked!

I got through the rest of my afternoon classes somehow, but that Monday just wasn't my day.

On my way home I pass an elementary school. In the yard there, I saw Ken Nakamura bullying a little girl. He had her shoulder and was trying to take a lollipop away from her. She was kicking at his shins.

"What do you think you're doing?" I asked.

The little girl had on a red jumper dress and white boots. Her jet black hair looked as though someone had put a bowl over it and then cut it, and one of her front teeth was missing. She surely was cute—but mad!

"Mind your own business, why don't you?" she yelled at me, as a good kick landed on Ken's shin. He let go of her shoulder, and she told me, "Leave us alone." Then she popped the lollipop into her mouth.

Larry Brunn is a dumb kid in my English class; the kind

of guy who always yells "Fight!" if two fellows have words. I didn't know he'd come up behind us until he began shouting. Besides yelling, this time he gave me a push.

I put out my hands to catch my balance, pushing Ken as I did so. He swung a wild punch that grazed my forehead, and I cocked my fist to hit him.

Suddenly there was a sharp pain in my right leg. The little girl had tossed away her lollipop, jerked up my pants leg, and was she biting! Her hair flew as she sank in her teeth. Boy, it hurt!

"Tishi, stop that!" Ken grabbed her shoulders.

I sat down on the sidewalk to pry her loose. It took both Ken and me to do it, too.

I was holding my leg when Tishi picked up her lunch box. She let me have it with a full arm swing that landed on my right eye.

When Ken got the lunch box away from her, he clamped on an armlock and said, "Pat, this is my little sister. Sorry about that whack. She's not supposed to have candy until after supper."

"What a tiger!" I sat on the curb, rubbing my leg with one hand, while I cupped my eye with the other.

Tishi's almond-shaped eyes stared at me. "You broke it." She showed me her lunch box.

Sure enough, the catch was sprung. "You didn't help my eye much, Tiger!"

"Me Tishi." She grinned. "Is okay. Ken fix him."

Ken put a hand down to help me up. Tishi got into the act, pushing me from behind. Walking down the street, she held my hand instead of Ken's.

"She likes you," he told me.

She bobbed her head when I looked down. "Tishi like."

Ken was staring at my eye. "That doesn't look good, Pat."

"From my side, it doesn't feel good, either, but I think I'll live. There should be a *Beware of Tishi* sign around her neck." I was limping slightly. "Has she had her rabies shots?"

Ken laughed. "Tell you what," he said. "Come up to our place over the restaurant. I've had first aid in Boy Scouts, and I'll patch that eye."

"All right, and while you're at it, maybe you can patch up a story for me to tell my family. They'll never believe a little kid banged me up."

Ken frowned. "You can't blame them. They don't know Tishi."

The Nakamuras, I found out, had just opened the new Sukiyaki Restaurant on Fisherman's Wharf. Dad sails from that wharf. Directly across the bay from Alcatraz Island, it's a big tourist attraction in San Francisco. People come from all over the world to eat crab, lobster, and fish in the more than a dozen fine restaurants clustered along the bay.

There are outside seafood stands, too, where you can get seafood cocktails and other things to eat right there or take home. There's a wax museum, and a penguin show. Many people come just to see the fishing boats anchored there, like Dad's *Macushla*.

I've been told there isn't another place in the world like Fisherman's Wharf, and I believe it. Excursion boats tour the harbor, and there's a lookout pier from which you can see the Golden Gate, as well as ships coming in and going out of the harbor. What it is, really, is a small city within a bigger one.

"We had another restaurant in Los Angeles before we came up here to Frisco," Ken explained, while he was working on my eye. Tishi had gone downstairs for her supper. "My older brother got married, so he and his wife run that one now. It's the way Japanese families do things."

"It sounds good."

"Japanese-American families," Ken corrected himself. "Dad and Mom get after me about this 'Japanese' thing."

When Ken finished cleaning my eye and daubing it with antiseptic, it looked awful, but felt better. "You do a good first-aid job," I told him. "Thanks."

"See you on the way to school tomorrow?" Ken asked before I left.

"I was going to ask you."

"I leave early, so I can drop Tishi off."

"Suits me. Eight o'clock? I was late today."

Ken grinned. "Eight's fine. Corner of Bay and Polk?"

"Good." I thought about Tishi. "Is she in school until we get out?"

"No. She plays in the school yard until I pick her up. With Mom and Dad always working, she's used to it, and so am I."

Dad and Jerry are usually in off the water by five, but this day they were home when I got there. That meant there had been a light catch of salmon. Dad was going to be in a discouraged mood. He was in the living room when I came into the house. He was rustling the *San Francisco Chronicle,* checking tide tables and fishing news.

Big Dan had the supper table set. I sniffed and found it was Irish stew tonight. When Big Dan cooks, that's usually what we have.

Megan wasn't due home until six.

Jerry was nowhere in sight. Mom was coming home on the bus tonight, so I thought maybe he'd gone to meet her. Dad doesn't like to drive in San Francisco traffic.

"Hi, there, Paddy," Dad said, as soon as he saw me in the doorway to the living room. I had my face turned so I wouldn't have to explain about the shiner yet. He stared at me over the top of his steel-rimmed reading glasses. "What has Number Two Son been up to all day?"

~~~~~~

CHAPTER 2

Dad and Jerry

⚓

I get that same question from Dad every night. "I haven't been up to much," I told him. That's the answer I give every night.

"Good." Dad rustled his paper. I could see he was upset about something. Absentmindedly he said, "You'd better go out to the kitchen and get something to eat."

Just then I heard Jerry thumping around upstairs. It sounded as if he was pulling the suitcase out of his closet. "Hi, Jer," I called up the stairs, as I went through the hall to the kitchen.

There wasn't any answer—just another thump.

"Hey, boy!" Big Dan noticed my shiner as soon as I stepped into the kitchen. He raised an eyebrow and whistled softly. "You can be proud of that one, Patrick. How did the other fellow make out?"

"It wasn't another fellow."

Big Dan considered that. "Girl?" he asked.

"If you have to know, yes. What's wrong with Dad?"

"Jim has to face up to the fact that his Number One Son isn't going to follow along in his footsteps. He'll get over it, and with no bones broken. I had to find out the same thing when he was Jerry's age. Are you hungry? It will be an hour before the stew is ready."

"I'm always hungry. Lunch was a disaster area today. What's for snacking?"

"Well, now, that's a good question."

"Oh, no! I almost forgot. Megan's doing the food shopping for us. Whatever there is in the fridge, want to bet it won't taste good but will be healthy?"

"No bet."

If we'd made a bet, Big Dan would have lost it. Megan is studying dietetics. That's how to feed sick people, I guess, although she denies it.

There was health bread, dark brown stuff that is chewy and tastes like sawdust and molasses. There was Melba toast, which I call shrunken bread. Instead of butter, the fridge was stocked with corn-oil margarine, which isn't bad, but it isn't butter, either.

There was vitamin-enriched skim milk, raisins, dates, and a lonely apple. I chose the apple. I don't like apples much, but it was the best choice out of that mess. "I hope Mom gets home before we all starve," I told Big Dan. "Do you think Megan will ever get over being a food nut?"

"In time, I expect," Big Dan said. "Her husband will see to that."

"Husband? Do you think Megan will ever get married?"

"It's something girls do, from time to time," Big Dan said. "Yes, I imagine she will."

"I can't picture that!"

Big Dan added a pinch of salt to his stew and stirred it. Just then Jerry slammed down the stairs. "Boy, does he sound mad!" I said.

Big Dan put a finger to his lips and cocked his head to hear what was being said in the living room. There was only silence for quite a while. Finally, Dad rustled the newspaper and we heard him say:

"Here, take the sports section."

"No, thanks," Jerry answered.

"Jerry . . ." Dad stopped. "All right," he then said in a gruff voice, "nothing much doing, anyway."

"Okay, so I'll read the sports."

"Storm brewing," Big Dan whispered to me. "Gale force, I'd say, wouldn't you?"

I nodded. "Good time to reef sails."

As Big Dan nodded, I said, "Hey, I goofed today—in English class."

"Is that why the girl hit you?"

"No." I touched my eye and winced. "Would you believe a little Japanese girl did this to me?"

"Of course not."

"I was afraid you wouldn't. Anyway, here's what happened. I was making a book report on that book you told me I should read, so I promised that I'd ask you to lecture us on the earthquake and fire. Mr. Morris, he's my teacher . . ."

"Hold up just a minute, Patrick. Let me get this straight. I'm supposed to lecture your English class?"

I nodded. "They're all good kids. Boy, does that beef stew smell great! You can really cook."

"Flattery won't do it, boy. Save your breath and blarney."

"All right I got trapped. Before I thought, I said I'd ask you." I shrugged. "I guess it's going to be all right if you say no. I'll explain that you're shy, or something like that. Or maybe your memory isn't so good any longer?"

Big Dan sighed. "Set the date, Patrick, and I'll be there with bells on."

Supper wasn't much fun that night. Megan came home and asked Dad and Jerry if anything was wrong. They both told her to be quiet.

She then chided Big Dan on the way he'd set the table. "The forks are supposed to be on the other side of the plates," she said. "Men have so much trouble setting a table."

"Now is that a fact?" Big Dan asked. "Those forks are all right where they are."

As soon as we sat down to eat, Jerry noticed my eye. "In a fight, Little Brother?"

"No."

Megan got all excited. "You should have that eye treated, Pat. Black eyes aren't funny. We have a case over at the hospital right now . . ."

Dad banged a spoon against his water glass. "None of that hospital shop talk at the supper table, Megan. You know better."

"Sorry, Dad."

"He should have a slice of beefsteak on that eye," Dad said to Big Dan.

"Too late, Jim. It's all in the stew. I think the boy will be all right."

"How did it happen, Paddy?" Dad asked.

"Well, there was this little Japanese girl, and she had a lunch box."

Dad flushed. "I don't appreciate your sense of humor tonight."

Megan giggled. "Did you try to steal her candy?"

"I didn't. But I thought another kid was doing just that."

Big Dan rescued me. "A boy shouldn't have to explain a black eye," he said. "It isn't in the Bill of Rights, of course, but maybe it should be. There was a time, Jim . . ."

Dad grinned sheepishly. "You're right. Sorry, Paddy. We'll say you got it from a little girl, and let it go at that."

I sighed with relief. "Thanks."

"Think up a better yarn next time," Jerry said. "Try the running-into-a-door bit."

"Okay, I will. Do people really believe that one?"

Jerry laughed. "No, of course not. What do you expect?"

"I expect it's easier to explain a black eye," I said, "than getting bit on the leg by a small Japanese girl, so I won't try it."

"Paddy, you're not making much sense," Dad said, with a frown. "Eat your stew before it gets cold."

"Yes, sir."

Megan picked that time to say to Jerry, "Why are you packing your suitcases?"

"I'm moving out."

Everyone stopped eating; no one said anything.

"Dad, I'm sorry," Jerry said. "Sure, you need me on the *Macushla*. John isn't getting any younger." John works aboard the *Macushla,* too, and has for many years. "I know I'm being selfish, but I just don't like fishing. It doesn't interest me in the least, and never has. I want to go to business college."

"Fishing is a family business, Jerry. I want there to be a *Costello & Son* one of these days." Dad's face brightened. "Why not right now?"

"No." Jerry shook his head. "You just don't understand!" He'd raised his voice. "This isn't because we got mad at each other today on the boat. We do that all the time lately. I hate fishing!"

"It's our living, Jerry."

"Not mine, it isn't!"

"That's enough." The tone of authority in Big Dan's voice stopped Jerry cold.

"Sorry," he muttered.

"You should be," Megan told him.

Jerry told her to shut up.

"I've said that's enough!" Big Dan really had a bite in his voice this time.

Megan got up from the table. *"Excuse me!"* she said and bolted upstairs.

Jerry wadded his napkin and rose from the table.

Dad hadn't been looking at Jerry. He'd been staring up at the ceiling. Now he did look at Jerry. "When do you plan to leave, son?" he asked seriously.

"After Mom gets home tonight." Jerry sat down again.

"Sorry about the shouting. It's a bad habit, especially in front of Pat."

"Oh, don't mind me," I said.

Jerry grinned. "We don't."

Dad grinned, too. Then he got serious again. "All right, Jerry. I suppose it's time for you to get out of the fishing business and find your way in the business world. I should have realized it before. Will you need any money?"

"No, I've been saving. This isn't a sudden deal. I'm already registered at San Francisco Business College for night courses. I've rented a room, and I have a daytime job."

"Doing what?"

"I've joined the Longshoreman's Union."

"That's hard work."

Jerry nodded. "But the pay is good."

Megan's funny. She gets her feelings hurt and storms up to her room, but she always comes back. I think she's afraid she'll miss something. She'd come back in time to hear Jerry say he was going to be a longshoreman.

"You be careful," she told him. "We have a case at the hospital . . ."

At that moment, the front door opened and closed, and Mom was in the dining room. Mom has what I've heard people call a "brisk manner." Dressed up for traveling, with her hair done, and with makeup on, she isn't just pretty—she's beautiful. "Pretty" is for around the house.

"I caught an early bus, Jim," Mom said, smiling at Dad. "After all these years, do you know something?" She slipped an arm around Dad's neck to kiss him. "You're the most exciting man I know!"

Dad was beaming. "Sure good to have you home, Kate. How's your sister?"

"Ornery. She always was the spoiled one in my family. How are you, Big Dan? Megan, how did you make out? Jerry, what are your suitcases doing in the front hall? Hello, Paddy."

"Hi, Mom," I said with a big grin.

"What about the suitcases?" she asked Jerry again. "I almost broke my neck over them."

"I'm moving out, Mom."

"Well . . ." She hesitated, caught Dad's eye, and then said, "Did you remember to pack your clean shirts? They were in the bottom drawer." She patted Jerry's cheek. Then she turned to Big Dan. "Is that beef stew I smell? I'm just about starved!"

Mom finally spotted my black eye. She touched a finger on it gently. "Nice," she said. "Should I ask how you got it—and about the other fellow?"

CHAPTER 3

~~~~~~~~~~~~~~~~~~~~~~~~~~~~~~~~~~~~

Dad, John, and Me

⚓

Jerry didn't show up at home for the next two weeks. He phoned Mom twice, and talked with Dad once, but that's all we heard from Jerry. I was so used to having him around that I missed him as much as Dad did. Besides, Jerry used to help me with my homework. He was sharp when it came to math, and he wasn't bad at English, either.

Jerry's short and stocky like Dad—they look alike, too. I think I take after Big Dan. He's tall and husky. I soon found out, after Jerry left, that Megan was also good at math, so I didn't miss Jerry only because I needed homework help.

To tell the truth—until he went away—I had looked forward to the day Jerry would leave home. That wasn't because we didn't get along. I just thought that if he did go, maybe then Dad would notice I was around. But I was wrong. Jerry being gone didn't make any difference—I was still Number Two Son in the Costello family.

Megan moved right into Jerry's room because it was bigger than her old one and faced the front of the house. She was real happy, and satisfied. Megan acted as if Jerry had never lived with us. I called her on it.

"Don't you miss him?" I asked.

We'd finished going over my English homework, which was about the Romantic poets.

"Miss who, Pat?"

"You've got his room."

"Hadn't you noticed? This is my room now."

"Megan, what's *wrong* with girls?"

She stared at me with her wide blue eyes. "Pat, whatever in the world?" She brushed her hand over the cowlick at the back of my head. "You'll grow up and leave here, too. Don't you know that? Mom and Dad were alone together before we ever came along, you know."

"Dad and Jerry haven't got along all this last year, have they?"

Megan frowned. "I haven't paid attention, but I guess not. Why do you ask?"

"Will Dad and I get along, do you think?"

Megan shrugged her shoulders. "Up to a point, Pat." She was very serious. "At the hospital . . ." She changed her mind about that. "It's this way," she said. "You're a person all by yourself, aren't you?"

"I guess I am."

"You are, and so is Dad."

"So what's that mean?"

Megan brushed her blonde hair back from her high, narrow forehead. "I wish I knew," she said. "I think it's going to have to creep up on you, though, as it did on Jerry. All right?"

"If you say so," I told her. "Thanks for the help with Keats, Shelley, and Byron."

"Any time. Pat?"

"Yes?"

"I'm Big Sister, Pat." Then she said, "Jerry talked with me about moving out to go to business college. He's never liked to fish. I told him it was what he ought to do; that he needed to be independent of his family and stand on his own feet. I don't know what Mom told him, but she knew what Jerry planned."

"What about Dad?"

"Jerry is doing what he should be doing—until he's drafted." She hadn't answered my question. "You'll have the same decision to make one of these days. Everyone has to be independent of his family, sooner or later."

"All right, Megan. But what about Dad?"

"Jerry has to live his own life. So do I, and so do you, Pat."

"Right now I miss Jerry around here. Dad does, too, and you know it."

"Don't you think *I* miss him?"

"Do you?"

"Yes."

I grinned at her. "That makes all of us."

The Embarcadero is the heart of San Francisco's waterfront. It stretches along the bay from Fisherman's

Wharf to the Ferry Building with its tall clock tower. The Embarcadero *is* San Francisco.

Long piers poke like fingers into the sparkling water of the bay, flanked by cargo warehouses built out into the bay. The Embarcadero, named by the Spanish when they settled San Francisco, swarms with ships loading and unloading stuff from all over the world.

Once upon a time the Barbary Coast was part of the Embarcadero. Thugs kidnapped seamen and sold them to shipmasters to serve aboard for years at a time. Big Dan clears his throat and blushes if you ask *him* about the Embarcadero in the days when the Barbary Coast was running wide open.

Today it's tame compared to then, I guess. The schooners, brigs, clipper ships, and iron-hulled four-masters carrying grain to England are gone. In their place are liners and freighters from Australia, Korea, Vietnam, Japan, Tasmania, New Zealand, England, France, and South American ports.

The smell is of salt water, rope, crating lumber, and oil, blended with the aroma of strong coffee from the twenty-four-hour restaurants and lunch stands serving sailors and longshoremen, ship's officers, and policemen.

Grace Lines, Pacific-Orient, Matson, Dollar Line— name almost any line, and you'll find its ships tied up along the Embarcadero. Taiwan, Pusan, New Orleans, Manila, Papeete, Baltimore, Honolulu, New York, Boston —it's hard to find any port on a map of the world that hasn't a ship tied up along the Embarcadero.

Ships put a lump in my throat and speed up my heart. From a salt-encrusted freighter to a liner that's as stately as a great lady, each has a personality, and I think of them as alive, crammed with memories as well as cargo.

I plan to make a career out of the Navy. Ken, I found out, has his sights set on the Merchant Marine. "One place you'll never find me, when I'm on my own," he told me, "is running a restaurant!"

It was Saturday morning. We had eaten breakfast at the Lighthouse Restaurant on Fisherman's Wharf, because we planned to spend the day bumming along the Embarcadero. Tishi was with Mrs. Nakamura that day, so not having to baby-sit had cut us loose.

We took our time, studying each ship in its berth. "What's your dad doing about your brother?" Ken asked me, while we walked along.

"What's to do about Jerry? He's moved out."

"Who's taking his place on the boat?"

"A fellow named Trembly. He was looking for a job, so Dad hired him, on a trial basis."

"Know something? You're crazy not to help your dad. What kid has a chance to go fishing every day, and draw wages for it besides? I'd go just for the boat ride."

"Dad hasn't asked me to help."

Ken glanced at me. "Is that what's bothering you? My dad *tells* me; he doesn't ask. I do all the asking. It's that way in a Japanese family. You ought to see."

That was all we said on the subject that day.

That night, when Dad came home, he looked more discouraged than ever.

When Mom asked what was wrong, Dad blew up.

"Trembly isn't going to work out, that's what's wrong. The man is lazy, Kate! He doesn't know a fish from a crab, either. I'm going to have to give him his walking papers."

"Jim, are you sure that you're not getting a little hard to get along with aboard the *Macushla?*" Big Dan asked.

Dad surprised me, and I think he surprised Mom. Instead of denying it, he said, in a moody voice, "Well, yes, I suppose I am. Jerry seemed to think so."

By the next Friday night, after hinting all week about looking for a full-time summer job, with no response from Dad, except, "That's a fine idea, Paddy," I decided a drastic move was up to me.

I checked with Big Dan about it. There's a small backyard behind our house with a brick wall around it. Big Dan likes to sit out there in the evenings. It was early, but Mom and Dad had already turned in, and Megan was out on a date.

I slipped downstairs to see Big Dan when I was sure Mom and Dad were asleep. On the way, I got a slice of cake and a glass of cold milk.

"Prowling tonight?" Big Dan asked, as I joined him in the backyard. He was smoking his pipe.

"Something like that."

"How's the cake?"

"Good."

"Your sister baked it."

"Are you kidding?"

Big Dan shook his head. "I'm not. After all the remarks you made about her cooking during the time Kate was gone, maybe you'd better compliment Megan's cake."

"I think you're right," I told him. "Big Dan?"

"What's on your mind?"

"I want to help Dad aboard the *Macushla*."

"Jim can use some help. He hasn't replaced Trembly, you know, and the boat is too much for him to handle with only John's help."

"So that's why Dad has been so tired every night this week."

"That's the reason. Kate's worried about him, and so am I."

"I'm going to do something about it."

Big Dan knocked the ashes out of his pipe and slipped it into his coat pocket. "What do you have in mind?"

"I'm going out on the *Macushla* tomorrow morning. If I can stick, when school's out at the end of next week, I'll have my full-time summer job."

"Do you think you can handle a man's job, Pat?"

"Tomorrow I'm going to find out. When Dad gets down to the boat, I'll be aboard, helping John. Maybe he'll put me back on the dock, but I have to find out."

"You've talked with him?"

"No. I'm afraid he'll say forget it."

Big Dan was thoughtful for a moment. "I think you're handling this the right way," he said then. "Jim would hesitate to take you out, certainly, after his experience with Jerry. A man doesn't like to be hurt twice for the same reason. There is one thing, though."

"What's that?"

"Fishing is hard, grueling work. Don't try it unless you have the guts to stick it out."

I set my alarm clock for three in the morning, but I woke up even before it rang. I sneaked Jerry's rubber boots and his slicker, and I skipped breakfast so I could get out of the house before Dad woke up.

The fishing boats sailing from Fisherman's Wharf are in a lagoon behind the restaurants. There are more than fifty of them, not counting the sport-fishing cruisers.

The *Macushla* is a typical San Francisco fishing boat. It's painted bright blue, and from the bows to the transom, or stern, it's only twenty-one feet long. There's a wheelhouse that is as large as two telephone booths forward, with a small storage cabin under the forward deck.

There's a two-way radio in the wheelhouse, a magnetic compass, controls for the four-cylinder Gray marine diesel aft, a box of flares, and an old kitchen chair. Behind the wheelhouse is the cockpit, with square, wooden boxes for the catch. The bait tank is behind the engine, and just ahead of the transom. That's all there is to the *Macushla*, and tourists think it's pretty dinky to sail outside the Golden Gate, but they don't know how seaworthy she is.

Dad bought the *Macushla* eighteen years ago. He named it that because we're Irish, and "Macushla" is his pet name for Mom.

John was already aboard when I came along the high dock over the boat slips and climbed down the ladder to the U-shaped piers. He was doing something to the engine.

John is sixty, with stooped shoulders and a wrinkled, leathery face. I don't know his last name, but it's Italian. A lot of the boat skippers along Fisherman's Wharf are Italian. He looked up when I stepped onto the boat.

"I'd guess you were Jim's Number Two Son," he said.
"That's right."

"Going to give fishing a try?"

I nodded. "Dad doesn't know about it yet, though."

"I see. Well, good luck."

"Thanks. I may need it. Dad doesn't like to be surprised."

Just then I saw him swinging along the high dock, whistling, and speaking to the other fishermen getting their boats ready to go out. He saw me before he climbed down the ladder. That stopped his whistling. He was frowning when he came down the ladder and stepped aboard.

John didn't look up from what he was doing to the engine, but he said, "He's a husky lad, Jim. We can use a strong back aboard."

"My thinking, too, John." Dad grinned at me, and then pushed his hand into his pants pocket. He gave me a dollar bill. "An advance on wages, Paddy. Get yourself the breakfast you didn't eat at home, and then call your mother, so she won't be worried. After that, hurry back."

"Yes, sir!" Everything was suddenly all right.

I didn't know that was to be the last time anything would be all right with me that day.

~~~~~~~~~~~~~~~~~~~~~~~~~~~~~

CHAPTER 4

Seasick

⚓

A twenty-knot wind was whipping the harbor. As soon as the *Macushla* poked her bows out of the lagoon, I was sorry I had eaten breakfast. I was supposed to be helping John get the fishing tackle organized.

"You'd better head for the stern, boy," he told me suddenly.

I just made it. John came scrambling back to grab me around the waist. If he hadn't done that, I would surely have gone overboard. My head was spinning.

"You'll feel better now," he said, when I'd finished throwing up.

John was wrong about that. Trying to tie a leader to a hook, I stabbed the hook into my thumb. By the time John had worked it out and applied antiseptic from the first-aid kit, I was sick to my stomach again.

After that, I had to lie down back in the cockpit. I was too dizzy to stand up, and my chest and stomach muscles were sore. My head began aching, and the taste in my mouth was awful. Outside the Golden Gate, the water was rougher yet, and spray soaked me. I began shaking.

As salmon approach rivers for spawning, they swim in large schools. When you get one strike, the rest of the school boils around to feed, and the action is fast. It was a good day for fishing, and Dad and John began yanking them in over the side. All I could do was crawl around, trying to stay out of the way of the fish. The smell didn't do me any good, either.

I didn't get a line wet all day. Going back in, John began gutting the fish we'd caught and throwing their insides back into the ocean. Sea gulls swooped down in our wake to feed, making a horrible racket that hurt my aching head.

I curled up in a corner of the wheelhouse, holding my stomach and groaning. Dad glanced down at me. "Do you think you'll make it ashore, Paddy?" He put a hand on my forehead to see if I had a fever. "If I hadn't thought you'd throw it off, I would have run you back in early this morning."

"You never should have let me come out!"

"It was your own idea, Paddy."

As soon as I was back on land, my headaches went away and my stomach felt only empty. I had a little trouble walking, because it felt to me as if the land was rocking, but by the time we reached home, I was over that. Mom asked me how it had gone as soon as I was inside the front door.

"You tell her the bad news," I said to Dad and went upstairs to lie down.

That night Megan told me I'd had *mal de mer*. "That's the French word for seasickness. It sounds better; it has more class," she explained.

"You be seasick in French. Who needs 'class'? Just tell me how *not* to be seasick."

"The best way to avoid *mal de mer*," she said with a straight face, "is to get off the boat and sit down under a shady tree."

"I come to you for help, and what do I get? Comedy! Do you write your own stuff? It's awful!"

Megan laughed. "Sorry, Pat. Seasickness is caused by the balance mechanism in your ears."

"My ears didn't hurt. Have *you* ever been seasick?"

"No."

"Oh, boy! Some expert I pick!"

"I know what to do about it, though."

"You've already done the 'shady tree' bit, so knock it off, Megan, will you?"

"I'm serious now, Pat. What you need is Dramamine. It's good for all motion sickness."

"Thanks, Megan."

"Are you going to try life at sea again?"

I nodded. "Dad can use me on the *Macushla*. He just doesn't know it yet."

"I don't know that I'd be that brave, Pat. Dad told Mom how sick you were. Only Big Dan thought you'd ever try it again."

"That's the trouble with being Number Two Son," I told her. "A guy's whole family sells him short."

Since Dad doesn't fish on Sundays, I'd have to wait until after school was out to try it aboard the *Macushla* once more. So on Sunday, Ken and I toured the Embarcadero again, only this time Tishi came with us.

She wanted to hold my hand, and would have nothing to do with Ken. When he started to pester her about it, I said, "Hey, it's all right. This way I'm sure she can't slug me with something."

"Ken fixed box," she said.

"She means her lunch box," he told me. "How did the fishing go yesterday?"

"I have fish." Tishi was staying with the conversation, regardless!

"She has a goldfish. Now, be quiet a minute," Ken told her.

She poked her tongue out at him.

"Pat wants to talk," Ken added.

"All right." She grinned up at me. "Talk, Pat."

"Thank you, Tishi." For a moment I thought I'd lie to Ken, but I didn't. "It was pretty awful. I got seasick, and Dad and John had to work around me all day. I just fouled everything up for them."

"Are you going to try it again?"

"Yes. Dad doesn't know it yet, but I am."

Ken sighed. "I sure wish I could get on that boat! I don't know why my mother and father like the restaurant business so much. It's just a stack of dirty dishes to me."

At Pier 23 they were unloading a Japanese freighter. She was named the *Manhattan Maru*. Deck-mounted cargo cranes were lifting wooden cases from the holds, swinging them over the pier, and then lowering them down to longshoreman crews. A scene like that is all action.

Every extra day a ship is in port costs the company thousands of dollars. Longshoreman have to work fast, and they do. There isn't any shouting or fuss—every man knows exactly what he's doing, and does it.

"My grandfather skippered a freighter," Ken said, while we were watching the Japanese ship being unloaded. "He went down with his ship during World War II."

"Jap or Nazi sub get him?"

"No, it was an American sub. One of ours. He was on a run to Saipan, before the invasion."

"Oh." I was sorry that I'd asked.

Ken wasn't. He wanted to talk about the war and his family. "Dad fought with the 100th Division and was wounded twice, at Anzio and in the fighting near Rome. He still limps—you may have noticed. Mom was just a teen-ager, then, but she was in a camp near Denver, Colorado. 'Dangerous alien,' they said. She laughs about it now." Ken grinned. "I don't know where I'd be, if the F.B.I. hadn't rounded up Mom and her folks, though."

"How is that?"

"Her folks met Dad's folks in that camp, and that's how he came to meet Mom, after the war."

"It sounds tough, just the same."

Ken shrugged. "War is tough." He pointed to a Japanese officer on the bridge. "I'll be up there one day, but on an American ship."

"Me, too," Tishi said. She was bored with not being in on the conversation. "Pat, do you have fish?"

"No, I have an older brother, instead," I kidded her. Then I remembered that Jerry's rented room was an address on Battery Street near Bush, close to the Ferry Building at the end of the Embarcadero. "Want to come meet my brother?" I asked Ken.

Ken wasn't so sure Jerry would be glad to see the three of us, but we went. His name was on one of the mail boxes at the foot of dingy stairs that led up into a five-floor building. Jerry's room was on the second floor. We let Tishi knock on the door.

"Come in, whoever you are, unless you want to borrow money," he sang out.

"Hi, Jerry." I went in first. "This is Tishi Nakamura and that's her brother Ken." Jerry was in his undershirt and slacks, studying at a desk made of a board resting on two upended crates. He was sitting on a nail keg, and a sagging bed was the only real piece of furniture in the small room. "Want us to go away? You look busy."

"I was, but I'm not now. I certainly don't want you to go away." Jerry got up and slipped into a shirt. "How's Dad?"

"He's all right, but pretty busy. I tried helping him on the boat yesterday, but it didn't turn out so well."

"Seasick?"

"How did you guess?"

Jerry laughed. "You couldn't have been any sicker than I was, my first time out. Stick with it and you'll be all right."

"I hope so. What if I can't fish, though?"

"You'll do it."

"I'll try, that's sure. How's school?"

"Keeping me busy. I planned to come home and see Dad before this, but you know how it is. I've had a lot of work on the piers, too."

"Why don't you come see Dad tonight?"

"I have a date."

"That isn't a good excuse."

Jerry grinned. "All right. I'll bring her."

That surprised me. Jerry always kept his romantic stuff Top Secret.

While we were walking back up the Embarcadero, Ken said, "You have a nice brother."

"He was just Old Jerry around home. Now it's a lot different. That sure is a crummy place he's living in!"

"He's just starting out. My brother lived in a worse dump for a while.

"I got dump truck," Tishi said.

We'd almost forgotten she was with us. To make sure that she wasn't forgotten again, she said, "Catch me, Pat," and bolted up the sidewalk.

"Hey, look out!" I yelled.

Looking back over her shoulder and laughing, Tishi was coming to a curb.

"You'll fall!" Ken shouted.

She did, head over heels. I expected some real squalling, but she got up, rubbed her knees, and bit her lower lip.

Ken caught up first. "Why did you do that, Tishi?"

She hauled off and kicked him in the shins.

"One of these days!" Ken jumped around on one leg, holding his shin. "Tishi . . ."

She threatened to kick his other shin, but I grabbed her first. "That's enough, Tiger."

Jerry showed up for supper and brought a Marilynn Bronson with him. She was small and cute, with dark hair, brown eyes, and a dimple in her right cheek.

Before supper was over, Jerry announced that they were engaged and would be married in mid-June. That brought all other supper conversation to a grinding halt!

Dad recovered first. "Well, now, Jerry, what about business college? You quit fishing to get an education, remember."

Marilynn was looking pretty miserable. It turned out that Jerry hadn't told her he was going to announce their engagement that night.

"Maybe I should be excused," she said. "I know you people will want to talk about this without me here."

"No, you stay, Marilynn." Jerry was getting red in the face. "All of you might as well know that I got my draft notice. I'm going to carry on my business studies by mail while I'm in the service."

"You can't marry a girl and run off and leave her right away," Dad said. "I won't . . ." He stopped.

Mom had warning glances shooting all around Dad. Big Dan kept shuffling his silver and clearing his throat. Megan said, "Dad, we have a guest."

"Hey, I think it's great," was my contribution. Someone

had to say *something* cheerful. "How many kids are you going to have?"

Big Dan exploded with laughter. Megan raised her napkin to hide behind it. Jerry stared at me as if he was about to explode all over the dining room. Mom had a terrible time keeping a straight face.

Dad grinned at Marilynn. "Young lady, I wish I'd asked that question instead of Paddy, and also instead of warming up the 'heavy father' bit. Will you excuse me?" Then he turned his grin on Jerry. "Congratulations, son. You two will make it fine."

~~~~~~~~~~~~~~~~~~~~~~~~~~~~~~~~~~~~~~~

CHAPTER 5

Big Dan Speaks

⚓

My grandfather has lived with us all of my life, but there were some things I didn't know about him until he spoke to my English class.

"When an earthquake rocked San Francisco at five in the morning on April 18, 1906," he began after Mr. Morris had introduced him, "I was shaving. I was due for an inspection and a twelve-hour tour of duty at six that morning. During the next forty-eight hours I watched Old San Francisco die."

His tone of authority hushed the class. "We oldtimers never refer to it as 'the Earthquake,' however. We'd had these before. What we hadn't had was a fire that would burn out the old San Francisco to make way for the new."

Then he told us what it was like. "Since the development of incendiary bombs in World War II, we know about 'fire storms,'" he said, "but broken water mains and the death of San Francisco's fire chief in the line of duty gave us a fire storm way back then. Do any of you by any chance happen to know what a fire storm is?"

Even Ken didn't raise his hand this time.

"Flames feed on oxygen. When it's all consumed, a vacuum results. More oxygen rushes in to fill it, and wilder flames result. That is a fire storm."

He told us how the "fireproof" buildings didn't, in fact, burn, but they exploded from the intense heat. And how the Army, Navy, and San Francisco's Fire and Police Departments blew up people's homes to create jagged fire-breaks.

Big Dan spoke about the people who had to flee ahead of the flames with only what they could carry. Then he said, "I'm proud and thankful to God I was there, because ever since then I've known what the *human spirit* is. You kids with relatives who went through 'the Fire' can be proud, too. I never heard a word of complaint or discouragement all the time I was on duty. All any of us cared about was the new San Francisco. We started building it while the ashes of the old one were still hot. As you'll notice, we're still building it today."

All of us filed out of that classroom prouder of San Francisco than we'd ever been before.

On Friday Marina Junior High let out for the summer. The following Monday morning I went out with Dad and John on the *Macushla* again. It wasn't easy to make myself do it. At the same time, I couldn't *not* do it.

Dad understood. "Come along aboard," was all he said when I asked him if I could go.

I skipped the pills Megan had got for me. I didn't want to depend on them.

The wind was strong, and the harbor was really kicking up. The *Macushla* bucked like a bronco as soon as Dad steered her out of the lagoon. I gritted my teeth and hung on, waiting for my stomach to take me back to the stern, but it never did.

Even the heavy following swells, outside the Golden Gate, didn't throw me. Dad trusted me with the helm. I soon had the "feel" of the *Macushla's* steering. My course was for Mile Rock, and I hit it on the button. That got me a pat on the shoulder from Dad.

Then I was in the cockpit with Dad and John, while the *Macushla* bobbed and drifted, hauling in salmon. They really hit. We forgot about bait and flipped the bare hooks back in the water. I learned to brace and heave whenever I got a strike, whipping the fish inboard with my legs, back, and arms.

I didn't notice a fog bank rolling in from the ocean. When we finally started in, the fog had almost caught us, and it succeeded in doing so before we reached the Golden Gate. I couldn't make out the bottom of the huge bridge span when we were directly under it.

Dad had the helm. John and I, with the catch gutted, huddled back in the cockpit. It was weird sliding through the sheets of fog, unable to see anything five feet away. Scary, too. Fog horns blasted all around us because we were in the steamer lane.

I asked John if he was scared.

"Not so long as Jim Costello has the wheel up there,"

he told me. "Jim will always get us to the slip, safe and sound. Watch and see."

Once Dad raised the hair on my head. A fog horn blasted off our starboard bows quarter. It sounded a long way off to me, but suddenly the *Macushla* was in reverse.

A moment later, a tug pulling a barge loaded with railroad cars cut directly across our bows.

The tug and barges cut across our course so close, dead ahead, that I could smell coffee boiling in her galley, and read the American Car & Foundry trademarks on the wheels of the railroad cars.

"Gets hair-raising, doesn't it?" I said to John.

He chuckled. "Stay aboard, boy, if you think that was close. We fishermen are the waifs of the sea. Some of the time, you'll swear all the other boats and ships are trying to run us down."

Walking home from Fisherman's Wharf, I asked Dad why he reversed the *Macushla*'s engine exactly when he did. "I thought that tug sounded a long way off our course," I said, "but you knew it wasn't. How was that?"

Dad pursed his lips, thinking how to answer my question. "Seamanship is many things a man can measure," he said finally. "It's also other instincts we can't measure, or even account for. When you've been at sea as long as I have, maybe you'll understand."

"You had *some* reason to hit the panic button. I would have sworn that tug and barge were a mile away and not cutting across our bows."

"Is that so?" Dad was interested. "Do you know, Paddy, I heard her out there exactly that way?"

"How did you manage to save our necks by doing what you did, then?"

"Instinct—and faith enough to depend on it. It's the real difference between a sailor and a landlubber."

"Will I ever have it?"

Dad said, "You'll be the first to know, if and when you do."

CHAPTER 6

~~~~~~~~~~~~~~~~~~~~~~~~~~~~~~~~~~~~~

Jerry's Accident

⚓

Ken wanted to get on board the *Macushla*. I didn't
know how to bring up the subject with Dad. You just don't
tell him, "Look, my best friend, this Japanese boy, wants
to be a fisherman."

Tuesday night the phone rang and Megan answered. I
was watching TV. Dad was doing his accounts, and Mom
was in the kitchen. Big Dan had gone for his evening walk
along Bay Street, and to take a ride on the Powell Street
cable car.

"Yes, this is the Costello residence," I heard Megan
say. Dad laid down his pencil. I switched off TV. Mom
stopped rattling dishes in the kitchen.

"Yes, yes, this is the Costello residence." Megan's voice
sounded high and strained.

Mom came from the kitchen, and Dad walked over
from his desk. "What is it, Megan?" he rumbled.

I stayed sprawled on the floor. A thought streaked through my mind—*Something's happened to Jerry*.

Megan said then, in a dead voice, "Thank you. We'll get there as quickly as we can. You did say San Francisco General Hospital? Yes, thank you." She put the telephone back on its cradle and turned slowly to face Mom and Dad.

"*What is it?*" Mom's voice was tight and demanding. "Tell us, Megan."

Rapidly Megan explained that Jerry had been hurt on the docks. It was his boss who had just called. Jerry was in surgery.

In no time at all, we were all in the family Chev, and Dad was driving us to General Hospital.

Mom took command. "As soon as we get there," she told Megan, "you phone Marilynn. Do you have her number?"

"No."

"She's in the telephone book," Mom said. "Don't forget, Megan."

"Yes, Ma." Her voice was tearful and she sounded no older than Tishi.

"Stop crying," Mom snapped at Megan. "Pat?"

"Yes?"

"Your brother's been badly hurt."

That didn't make much sense. Mom knew I knew that, but I said, "Yes, Mom."

Dad was driving well. Even though he hates to drive a car in the fast-moving San Francisco traffic, right now he was booting the family Chev along like a contestant for the Grand Prix.

"I need you so much now," was all Mom said to Dad. I saw her profile as she stared toward him. It put a bigger lump in my throat than the one already there.

Dad took one hand off the wheel to pat Mom's shoulder. "I've been here all these years, Macushla."

A strangled sound came from Mom, and she moved closer to Dad.

Megan started sobbing.

"Quit it," I told her. "That won't help."

The name of Jerry's boss was Mike Standish. He was a huge, fat man, with a fringe of red hair around an almost bald head. He smelled like the piers. "A bale brushed your boy off a truck," he told Mom and Dad when he met them in the reception room. "He'll be out of surgery soon. Blast those treacherous docks!"

"Somebody has to keep the cargo moving, especially to our armed forces in the Far East." It was Dad who said that. "This isn't your fault."

Mr. Standish blinked. "Thanks, Costello. I'm glad you realize that."

"How badly is Jerry hurt?" Mom asked.

Megan stood there, wringing her hands, with tears streaking her cheeks.

"Some nurse you're going to be!" I said to her hotly. I didn't mean to be nasty; the fact that I was as afraid for Jerry as she was made me react that way.

Mr. Standish spoke slowly. "Mrs. Costello, we don't know yet, but he had a nasty fall. His right arm is broken. Some ribs, too. It's possible head injury that bothers the doctors most."

At that moment, Marilynn came into the reception room. Marilynn lived in Oakland. Megan had called her at her home in Oakland as soon as Dad parked the car. Marilynn walked directly to Mom, and they put their arms around each other.

"Want a Coke?" I asked Megan. There was a dispensing machine in the corner. Megan shook her head.

The hospital's piped music system was playing a song titled "Be Happy Tonight." I wondered who the clown was who put on *that* record?

A doctor in a green gown, with a mask hanging around his neck, came into the reception room. "Mr. Costello?" At Dad's nod, he went on, "Your boy is going to be all right. It will take his arm a while to heal, but there's no head injury after all. The ribs were cracked, not broken. You've a tough-bodied kid there."

Jerry came home on Friday. The Army delayed his induction until late July, and he and Marilynn postponed their wedding until early in July.

It was good to have Jerry home, and I got a chance to talk with him about some things that were beginning to bother me.

"I never knew that fishing was such a tough way to make a living," I told him one night when we were yakking together. "If you're not cold out there, you're wet—usually you're both cold and wet. I still get seasick once in awhile, too. Will I ever get over that?"

Jerry laughed. "You may, but I never did. I've seen Dad and John feed the sea gulls, too, so don't let it bother you."

Then we talked about sport fishing. Sport-fishing day boats sail from the lagoon at Fisherman's Wharf. These are bigger boats than those used by the commercial fishermen. With twenty or thirty sport fishermen aboard, they go out after salmon.

The boats have cabins with bunks, galleys for coffee and sandwiches, ship-to-shore phones, and most of the trimmings you find on pleasure boats.

When Dad mentions the skippers of these boats, he calls them "White Collar Fishermen," and he doesn't seem to have much use for them. I'd noticed, though, that most of their skippers drove big cars and didn't seem to have any money problems.

"Hey, what's Dad got against people like Skipper Bob, Skipper Dan, and Skipper Lew?" I asked Jerry now. Sport-fishing skippers give their names this way in their newspaper advertising and on their boats.

Jerry scowled. "We're talking about our father, Pat."

"I know. Isn't that all right to do?"

"Up to a point, yes. We keep it off the record, though."

"Okay."

We were upstairs in Jerry's bedroom. He grasped his knees with his good arm. "Rub my back, will you?"

"Sure."

Jerry sighed. "That sure feels good!"

"What were you going to say about Dad?"

"He's the best commercial-fishing skipper sailing from Fisherman's Wharf. You probably know that already. If you don't, John will tell you, and he's right."

"John's told me, but I knew it, anyway."

"Dad can find salmon if there are any down there to

find. He watches for undersized fish like a hawk, and he's completely fair in all his dealings with wholesalers. In addition, he's a top-notch boat skipper."

"I know *all* that."

"The *Macushla* isn't in too good shape. The engine needs an overhaul, and she's leaking too much. Ask John, he'll tell you."

"I don't have to ask him. Dad and I hear from him about the *Macushla* every morning when he cranks it up! Why doesn't Dad buy a new boat?"

"Money, why else? There isn't enough of it in salmon fishing any more, and that's the only commercial fishing up here in San Francisco, except for the crabbers and a few shrimp boats."

"Why doesn't Dad go into sport fishing, then? I asked him that just the other day, and he wouldn't even answer me."

"Money, again. Look, Pat, it takes money to make money. You always have to remember that. With our father's reputation, he could get backing—from a bank, say —to buy a new sport-fishing boat. I've quarreled with him about that. He got so that he wouldn't answer me, either."

"Is that why you quit the *Macushla?*"

Jerry shook his head. "No. Since I was hurt, I've had a chance to think about that, Pat. I should have confided in Dad when I first wanted to go to business college, instead of hitting him with it all at once after we'd had words aboard the *Macushla*. I put him in a rotten position. You live, and you learn—if you're smart."

"I've heard that somewhere before."

"You can stop rubbing my back now. Thanks a lot."

"You're welcome."

Jerry eased back on his pillows.

"Is Dad just stubborn about not going over into sport fishing?" I asked.

Again, Jerry shook his head. "He's stubborn, all right, but that isn't his reason, as I see it. You've mentioned Skipper Bob and some of the other sport-fishing skippers. They're men who are used to meeting the public, and most of them went to high school, at least. Dad's afraid he can't fit in with the type of people you get aboard a sport-fishing boat."

"You mean he feels inferior? Oh, boy! You get all kinds of people on those boats. You ought to see them."

"I have," Jerry told me. Then he seemed to change the subject and asked me, "Do you know Dad brags about the way you're helping him this summer?"

"No. All he does is complain about the way I do things on board the *Macushla*."

"Would you rather he went around telling you how much help you are?"

"Well, no."

"Settle then, and cut your losses, as they say in business college. But you can do Dad a favor."

"What's that?"

"Keep after him about sport fishing. It's what he ought to be doing. There's one thing about our father you should know."

"What's that?"

"Skipper Jim is going to be the best one sailing from

the lagoon at Fisherman's Wharf, if he ever makes up his mind to switch over from commercial fishing. Dad is like that, you may have noticed."

"You mean that he won't settle for less than being the best ever?"

"You have the message." Jerry grinned. "Just hope we were lucky enough to inherit that trait from him."

CHAPTER 7

~~~~~~~~~~~~~~~~~~~~~~~~~~~~

Trouble Aboard

⚓

Salmon are spawned in fresh water, up near the headwaters of certain rivers, but then they swim downstream to become salt-water fish. When they have grown to maturity, they somehow find the mouth of the river where they first swam into the ocean. They follow it upstream until they find where they were spawned. The female lays her eggs, the male fertilizes them, and then both fish die.

The Sacramento River feeds into San Francisco Bay. Huge numbers of salmon spawn at the headwaters of this river, swimming up rapids, jumping up low waterfalls, using fish ladders to get around dams, but before they can enter the Sacramento River, they must first swim through the Golden Gate.

Ships have to navigate the Golden Gate before they can enter the bay. This makes commercial salmon fishing a chancy thing. On clear days, it isn't too hard to keep a lookout and steer clear of ships coming into the Golden Gate, but when it's foggy, it's a mighty tough proposition.

Ships can't turn out for small boats. From the high bows of a ship, a lookout usually can't sight the fishing boats so far below him, wrapped in fog. The worst part is that ships have run down fishing boats without even knowing it—until later. It's something every fisherman has on his mind when the fog rolls in.

June was foggy,. but salmon were running, and Dad was after a record catch each time we went out. We got out first each morning and dragged in last nearly every afternoon.

John, I found out, had arthritis, and the dampness, plus the harder work, weren't doing him much good. "Are you after every salmon that ever spawned up around Sacramento?" he asked Dad once. "You're getting greedy, Jim."

"The time to fish most is when the fishing is best," Dad told John. "An oldtimer like you should know that."

John tapped his forehead. "I know that up here, but the old body doesn't."

"You're as good a man as you ever were," Dad said in a hearty voice.

He wasn't very hearty, though, when we came in off the ocean and got home at night. After he'd poked at the food on his plate long enough to satisfy Mom, Dad would go up to bed.

Big Dan finally got after him. "Trying to kill yourself, Jim?" he asked one night when Dad almost fell asleep at the supper table.

"No, and what makes you say something like that?"

Dad snapped at him. "You worked some pretty long hours when you were my age, I seem to remember."

Big Dan nodded. "True enough, and some of the corpses I met were heart-attack victims, or men who just died from pure overwork. If there hadn't been so many of them, I might have been able to get more sleep."

"We need the money," Dad said gruffly.

Mom wouldn't let him get away with that. "Those words will look very nice carved on a grave marker!"

Dad threw down his napkin and left the table.

Big Dan went on eating.

"What am I going to do with Jim?" Mom asked him.

"I used to wonder the same thing," Big Dan said. "He has a stubborn streak, as you've surely noticed."

"I've noticed," Mom said, "and I think I know exactly where he and Jerry got it."

I was worried about Dad's health, too, but he wasn't the one who broke down. We were in the steamer lane late one afternoon, early in July. We had a full catch aboard. Fog had closed in around us half an hour ago.

We were moving along slowly when Skipper Bob's sport-fishing boat suddenly loomed out of the fog, aimed at us amidships, and moving along at fifteen knots.

John had the helm because Dad didn't like the sound of the engine and was tinkering with it. I was posted as lookout. "Full astern," I told John, as soon as I saw Skipper Bob's boat.

In the excitement, John throttled up before he shifted into reverse. He said, later, that his hand was hurting from arthritis and he lost his grip on the shift lever.

Skipper Bob had thrown his boat hard to port, so a quick back-off would save a collision.

The *Macushla* lurched astern, all right, and just in time for Skipper Bob's *Rover* to cut across her bows, but the strain on the engine was too much. The crankshaft snapped, and we were drifting.

Dad got on the radio. Skipper Bob circled back to tow us in. He said he was sorry about the whole foul-up. Dad told him to forget it, but I heard him say to John, while we were in tow, "These sport fishermen think they own the ocean!"

"I'm about ready to let 'em have it," John grumbled. Standing beside Dad in the wheelhouse, he sucked on the stem of his pipe. "Jim?"

"Yes, John?"

We were just passing under the Golden Gate Bridge, and John stared up at it. "I won't see you again," he said under his breath. Then he spoke to Dad. "Jim, I'm quitting you and the *Macushla*. She'll be laid up now long enough for you to find a new hand. Do you remember my son?"

Dad nodded.

"He has a ranch in Nevada now, and a wife I don't know, as well as a grandchild I've never seen. They've been writing me to come up there. Jim, I'm going to go. I don't like to do this to you—we've been shipmates for fifteen years."

"Sixteen, John." Dad's voice was strangely gentle. "You came aboard a year before Paddy, here, was born."

"Sixteen, is it? It doesn't seem that long."

"Maybe that Nevada sun will help your aching bones."

John sighed. "I doubt it, but it's worth a try. And there's the grandson I've never seen. Thing like that pulls on a man, Jim. You'll know someday."

"Yes, I will, John."

John chuckled. "We've had fine times, Jim, as well as those that weren't so fine."

They'd forgotten I was aboard. "We've caught a lot of fish, John."

"That we have. We've put food on people's plates by taking it from the ocean for them, and they never knew us, but in a way we broke bread with them just the same. I'll think about that in Nevada."

"You'll come back to visit?"

John shook his head. He was staring at the San Fran-

cisco skyline as it twinkled in the early dusk. Lights were winking on in the tall apartment buildings that rise from Russian and Nob hills.

Buoys clanged faintly, and fog horns bleated, but the fog was now only mist over the land.

Dad was warping the *Macushla* into the lagoon. "I'm going to miss you, John. You will give us a thought from time to time, won't you?"

"You'll have many of them from me, Jim." John was blinking.

A lump was rising in my throat.

"Sorry we weren't shipmates longer, Paddy." John gave my shoulder a pat. "Take care of this sentimental Irishman, will you?" he said, winking at me and nodding toward Dad.

The *Macushla* was in her slip. John jumped ashore with a quicker step than I'd seen him use before. "So long, Jim—and Paddy," he said cheerfully.

Then, with a wave, he was gone.

After a while, Dad said, "Come on, Paddy. Let's clean up the boat. Tomorrow she goes in drydock, just like John."

While we were working, he said, "That wasn't a very funny remark of mine, was it?"

I didn't try to answer that one. Instead, I said, "My friend, Ken Nakamura, might make a good fisherman. I think he'd like to try it anyway."

"You mean to replace John?"

"Yes."

Dad shook his head. "What I don't need right now," he said, "is another green kid on board."

"All right, so I'll shut my big mouth." I went ahead with sloshing down the decks, but I was burning. Green kid! *When the Macushla makes it out of drydock,* I thought, *you're going to be short another "green" kid!* No more *Macushla* for me.

Dad let me fume for a while before he said anything. When we had the boat clean and were up the ladder, he put an arm around my shoulders. "Take it easy, Paddy."

"I am."

Dad sighed. "Do you know that I'm proud of the help you've been giving me?"

"No, you've never mentioned it."

We started to walk home.

"Not to you, I guess," he said. "Your mother knows it, and so does Big Dan. They're as proud of you as I am. Jerry and Megan know and are on your side, too."

I didn't say anything.

"Tell you what," Dad said, as if he'd suddenly had a good idea. "Why don't you have this Ken talk with me? If he can do half as well as you have so far, we'll have a full crew on the *Macushla* again."

"You're not kidding? Putting me on, or anything like that? Ken's my good friend, you know."

We stopped walking and faced each other. Dad took my shoulders in his big hands. "I'm neither kidding nor putting you on, Paddy. Is everything all right with you and me?"

I grinned at him. "It sure is!"

CHAPTER 8

~~~~~~

Sport Fisherman

⚓

The captain of the Port of San Francisco Harbor has his headquarters on Fisherman's Wharf. Dad wanted to lay up the *Macushla* at Hollister Ship & Boat Repair. This yard is down the bay from the Embarcadero, near the Naval Shipyard on Hunter's Point. Captain Daugherty of the Coast Guard, who's acting captain of the Port, had a work party taking one of the rescue motor launches to Hunter's Point, so they towed the *Macushla* to the Hollister yard.

The *Macushla* was winched up on the small-boat ways, with her hull entirely out of the water. It was encrusted with barnacles. Mr. Hollister and Dad were old business acquaintances—Dad had bought the *Macushla* second hand from Mr. Hollister.

He shook his head after he'd checked the hull. "Can't tell until she's scraped," he said to Dad, "but you may have a few seams that need recaulking. Has she been leaking?"

"Some. There are two or three inches of water in the bilge each morning. That's more than usual," Dad told him.

The Hollister engine mechanic had been checking the *Macushla*'s diesel. "It isn't too badly torn up," he reported, "but it should have a complete overhaul."

Dad's face got longer and more glum. "How much time and money to put the *Macushla* in shape?" he asked Mr. Hollister. "This is the height of the fishing season, you know. My family's bread and butter depends on that boat."

Mr. Hollister had to do some figuring on the back of an envelope. "To do the job right," he told Dad, "we need two weeks and roughly seven hundred dollars."

Dad whistled in surprise. "That much, and that long?"

"I'm afraid so, Jim. You can check around at some of the other repair yards if you want to. They might be able to shade my price, but you won't get the *Macushla* back in the water any sooner."

"I don't do business that way," Dad told him. "Go ahead and do the work."

We rode back to Fisherman's Wharf on the bus.

"When we're back in action," Dad told me on the bus, "you'll have a shipmate. I liked your friend."

Ken had come over to the house the night before for a talk with Dad. I didn't sit in with them.

"Gee, thanks!" I said.

Dad shrugged. "Don't thank me. Ken will earn his wages."

It had taken all morning and part of the afternoon to lay up the *Macushla*. When we got back, Skipper Bob was in and waiting to see us.

Skipper Bob is a sandy-haired man, sunburned brick red, who always wears a dark-blue yachting cap pushed back on his head. He talks fast and loud in a voice that sounds like gravel. Dad doesn't like him much.

"How long will you be out of the water, Costello?" he asked Dad.

"A couple of weeks, if you're really interested."

Skipper Bob chuckled, but he said, "Sorry about that. You look tired, though, and as if you could stand a little time off the water. I hear your Number One Son is getting married in a couple of days." Dad hadn't had a chance to edge in a remark yet. Before he could try, Skipper Bob went on to say, "Do you mind if I put a proposition to Number Two here? Temporary, of course, until you need him on the *Macushla* again. One of my deck boys just quit. I want Paddy, here, to pitch in and help me out."

"As far as work is concerned, Paddy is his own boss," Dad finally managed to say. He walked off to leave Skipper Bob and me alone.

"How about it, kid?"

I winced at the "kid," but I wanted a crack at sport fishing badly enough to put up with almost anything. "Call me 'Pat' instead of 'kid' and you have a deal."

"Check in at four tomorrow morning at my bait shop." Skipper Bob has a bait and tackle shop on Fisherman's Wharf where his customers congregate before going aboard the *Rover*. "You can learn the ropes aboard from my other deck boy."

With a pat on my shoulder, Skipper Bob strode off. I caught up with Dad. "Did you make a deal?" he asked.

"Yes, sir. Holy Toledo! I'll miss Jerry's wedding. What do I do about that?" I was to be an usher.

"Jerry's likely to forgive you," Dad said, "so long as his bride shows up."

"I think you're right," I told Dad. "Anyhow, I'll apologize to Jerry tonight."

"After he hears what you're going to do instead," Dad said, "I think he'll accept your apology."

"Get with Skipper Bob and learn everything you can about sport fishing, Pat," Jerry said, when I asked if it would be all right for me to skip his wedding. "We'll make it to the altar without your help."

The next morning, Skipper Bob bought my breakfast at the food bar in his bait and tackle shop. Fifteen men and four women were waiting to go aboard the *Rover* at daylight. They were eating breakfast, too, muffled up in sweaters, jackets, and scarves. Their cars were parked in the lot behind the shop. From the license tabs on the cars, I noticed that half of these people were from out of state. One car had a Florida license plate.

"Your job on board is to be helpful and courteous at all times, kid—I mean, Pat," Skipper Bob told me while I was eating. "You'll have to teach a few of them how to fish. Others will want you to bait their hooks. You'll land their fish for them with the net. We don't use a gaff, unless we have to, because it bloodies the water and draws sharks."

Skipper Bob finished his second cup of coffee. "Let me put it this way; we want everyone aboard today anxious to go fishing with us again."

Paul Beatty, the other deck boy, was on board when Skipper Bob led me and his guests out to the lagoon. Paul was a slender fellow of about Jerry's age, with dark-brown hair and a friendly grin.

"Once in a while we get a grouch," Paul told me, "or some feather head who thinks he knows more about sport fishing than Zane Grey did, but most of our customers are great people."

"I always thought Zane Grey wrote western novels."

"He did that, too, but he's written the best 'how to fish' stuff *ever* written, in my opinion. He just about invented sport fishing, you know."

The *Rover* was twin-engined with a fiberglass hull, about twice as long as the *Macushla,* and capable of twenty-five knots to the *Macushla*'s fifteen with her diesel putting out for full speed ahead. Skipper Bob opened the throttles and kept them open as we shot up the Marin County coast for the mouth of the Russian River.

"Salmon have been hitting in droves up there," Paul explained. "When people have paid the price to go out after fish, a sport-fishing skipper better find some!"

It was a bright, sunny morning, with clouds banking to the north. California 1 is a cliff-hanging road that skirts the Marin Peninsula's west shore. We could see car windshields blinking at us from along this highway.

We passed two shrimpers working Bodega Bay from Sausalito, a town across the harbor from Fisherman's Wharf. "There's a fellow planting oyster beds in there now," Paul told me. "He lowers them on racks, so bottom-feeding fish can't feast on his crop, and in three years he has a million dollars' worth of eating oysters."

On the last reach for the mouth of the Russian River, Paul and I started helping the people to unlimber their tackle. A lot of them used tackle rented from Skipper Bob.

One tall, bald man—a Mr. Lew Archer—had a green fiberglass rod and a special reel. He rigged his own leader to the light nylon line and fixed on it a feathered jig, instead of using live bait.

"Watch him, Pat," Paul whispered. "He'll show you how they do it in Florida. This is the third time he's been out, with a different rig every time."

"Can he fish?"

"He's an expert. Watch him and see."

Even though I was busy with the other customers, I kept a close watch on Mr. Archer.

In a few minutes, as the *Rover* idled along, Paul and I dipped handfuls of live bait out of the bait tank and tossed them over the stern. This method of raising fish to the surface to feed is called "chumming."

"Hook up!" A stocky man from Chicago jerked his rod to set the hook. "He's a big fellow!"

A lady shrieked. She'd hooked into a salmon, too. Two men hooked the same fish. Skipper Bob had to come back and cut them both loose. At one time it seemed as if everyone aboard was trying to land a fish at the same time. I'd just netted a beauty aboard for a woman when Mr. Archer's reel screamed right behind me.

"I've got a big lunker," he told me when I looked around.

"Net." The man from Chicago had his fish in close to the boat.

I jumped to help him, but the salmon spit out the hook

just as I lifted him. With a powerful flip of his body, he turned the net handle in my hands and spilled into the ocean.

"Pat, watch it! Be careful netting those fish!" It was Skipper Bob yelling at me from the bridge.

"Don't blame the kid," the man said. "He's doing his best." Out of the side of his mouth he told me, "I hate a man who yells at his help."

The salmon sounded as suddenly as they'd risen to feed. Only Mr. Archer was still hooked up. His fish was out there tail-walking, and he *was* a lunker!

"That one will go fifty pounds if he's an ounce, Archer," Skipper Bob called. "Play him cagey."

Paul sidled over to me. The clouds had shut out the sun. "Sharks get active with the sun under," he told me. "Something spooked that school we were in."

Skipper Bob was nervous, and I saw him pick up his .30–.30 shark rifle.

Mr. Archer was fighting his fish to a finish, snubbing him sooner on each run the salmon made.

"You have him tiring," Skipper Bob said. "Better bring him in, Archer. Our shark luck isn't going to hold much longer."

"Net, Pat." Mr. Archer had his fish trailing toward the boat now. "Help him heave, Paul."

Paul didn't move. "Look!" He pointed.

The gray shark showed his belly, smashing in to take the salmon on Mr. Archer's line. His first bite cut the salmon neatly in half. Mr. Archer reeled frantically, trying to land at least the front half of his salmon, but I guessed it wasn't going to be that way. The shark circled lazily, rolled again, and Mr. Archer had no fish at all. No *salmon*, that is.

The shark had taken the rest of the fish—*and* the hooks. Mr. Archer now had a shark to fight.

"Cut loose, Archer," Skipper Bob called from the bridge. "You don't want him."

But Mr. Archer wasn't about to cut the shark loose. He set his jaw. "Take my fish, will you?" he shouted. He gave the line a vicious yank. "You've had it, friend!"

CHAPTER 9

~~~~~~~~~~~~~~~~~~~~~~~~~~

Shark Bait

⚓

The shark didn't even feel the hooks! He started swimming away, but Mr. Archer jerked his rod double and set the hooks deep in the shark's gullet. It was a battle royal from then on.

Mr. Archer didn't have much chance. He was working with light tackle and the shark was a 300-pounder. "He may smash my tackle," Mr. Archer said through gritted teeth, "but it's going to be only after he's had a fight on his hands."

Instead of rushing, the shark began swimming a slow circle around the *Rover*, close in. He was just under the surface. Skipper Bob got into the act, taking pot shots from the bridge. The slugs slammed into the shark but didn't seem to bother him.

Mr. Archer kept working his circles closer to the boat. The shark slowly came alongside, and Skipper Bob had to stop firing. Mr. Archer asked Paul for a gaff. Paul went below decks and came back with a wicked-looking one.

After giving me the rod to hold, Mr. Archer leaned over the side to jab the shark with the barbed point of the gaff. He aimed for the gill slits.

"Don't try that!" Skipper Bob yelled from the bridge, but he was too late.

The shark rolled wildly, as Mr. Archer gaffed him. The handle of the gaff caught him under his left arm and lifted him overboard. As he rolled away, the shark snapped the line.

The *Rover* was drifting ahead, so when Mr. Archer bobbed to the surface, he was in the wake of the boat. The shark was now off our stern port quarter. His own blood in the water had maddened him.

Skipper Bob threw the *Rover* into a circle to starboard to pick up Mr. Archer, but he wasn't going to be in time.

"Hold it steady!" I yelled forward.

Skipper Bob couldn't see very well what was going on. He accepted my order, reversing the engines to stop the boat and hold her in position.

"Help me!" I shouted to Paul.

The fish the people had caught were drifting in a second tank aboard, to keep them fresh. I hauled out a big one and heaved it overboard, so that it splashed down between the shark and Mr. Archer.

The shark smashed at the fish. Paul got the idea right away. In rapid succession we threw overboard the boat's entire catch, as Mr. Archer swam for the stern of the boat. The shark was distracted enough to give him just time

to make it. Paul grasped one of Mr. Archer's arms while I grabbed his other one, and we hauled him back aboard.

Skipper Bob was astern by this time, with the shark rifle. He slammed a full clip of bullets into the shark, who was tiring fast now that he'd hit everything in sight except Mr. Archer. With a last flop of his tail, he rolled over on his back to float belly up.

"That was as foolish a thing as I've ever done," Mr. Archer admitted to Skipper Bob and the rest of us. "I hate sharks so much I guess it went to my head." He was shaking.

Skipper Bob told him there were some spare dry clothes in a locker below decks.

"Help me find them, Pat," Mr. Archer said to me.

I went below with him. I had the shakes, too, by this time.

"You used your head back there on deck," Mr. Archer told me while he was changing. "Did you ever see that trick done before?"

"No, sir. It just seemed to be a good idea."

"How old are you?"

"Fourteen."

He gave a sheepish grin. "This is the first time someone has had to save my life. I want to know all about the kid who did it. What do you do when you're not doing this? Besides going to school, I mean."

I told him about Dad being a fisherman, and how the *Macushla* was laid up right now. "I took this job to learn about sport fishing," I explained. "My brother Jerry and I want to get Dad off the *Macushla* and into sport fishing for a living."

"Do you think you can switch him over?"

"We haven't had much luck so far. Dad's stubborn."

"I'm a stubborn man myself," Mr. Archer admitted. "I'd like to meet your father. Will you introduce me if I give you a lift home?"

"Sure. Dad will be glad to meet you."

"I'm out here setting up a new plant in Petaluma to manufacture a new line of products for my Florida company," he told me. "Next fall we're bringing out fishing rods and reels under the Archer trademark."

Driving from Fisherman's Wharf to our house on Bay Street, Mr. Archer told me more about himself. "Back in Florida, at Tampa, I have a new sport-fishing boat, the *Amberjack*. I need a San Francisco skipper to bring it through the Panama Canal and up here. It's a company boat used for experimenting with various rods and rigs."

When we got to the house, we found Dad sitting on the front porch. After giving me too much credit for saving his life, Mr. Archer had a proposition for Dad. "If you'll get the *Amberjack* out here for me, taking your own crew, I think you may be the man I'm looking for to command the *Amberjack*. We can haggle about salary, but it will probably be more than you clear in commercial fishing. Are you interested?"

I surely was! I was excited enough to jump up and down, but I didn't, which was probably a good thing, because Dad said, "No, I'm not, thank you very much, Mr. Archer."

I groaned.

Dad shot me a sharp look. "I've been my own boss for

too long," he told Mr. Archer, "to start taking orders from someone else—more money or less money."

That night I asked Dad if being his own boss so long was the real reason he'd turned down Mr. Archer. The *Amberjack* was a forty-five-footer with gasoline-powered twin engines. She was fully equipped with magnetic as well as gyro compass, radar, loran, and every other navigational aid. She slept four. Mr. Archer had told me all this.

"If you're worried about navigating or handling a boat that size," I told Dad, "we could enroll in the school for power-boat skippers. You, Ken, and I could bring the *Amberjack* out all right."

Dad had been reading the paper. Now he laid it aside. "I've had quite a few years of practical experience in handling boats, Paddy," Dad said patiently. "When I first bought the *Macushla*, I was ambitious to skipper a larger boat one day, so I went to school at night and learned celestial navigation. Not that I don't appreciate your suggestion."

"I just thought I'd make it. I didn't know you'd studied navigation."

Dad grinned. "It surprises most boys, at your age, to learn their fathers aren't completely ignorant." Then he became serious. "I know you'd like me to take the job Mr. Archer offered, and I'm sorry to disappoint you, Paddy. We'll miss a fine boat ride, but when a man has worked all his adult life to stay independent, he doesn't like to throw in the sponge."

"I think I understand that."

"If you don't now," Dad said, "someday you will. How was it with Skipper Bob today?"

"All right, and I like sport fishing—for a change. You could do a better job of it than he does, though. As good a one anyway."

"Why is it that Number One and Number Two Sons both know what I can do better than I myself know?"

"Maybe because we're right?"

Dad laughed. "There's that possibility, but it isn't probable."

"Dad, this is the first really serious discussion we've had since I ran off from home when I was six, and managed to get only three blocks away."

Dad didn't say anything for a moment. "You startle me with that statement, Paddy," he said finally in a thoughtful voice. "Maybe we'd better not let it be so long before the next time."

"I hope we don't."

The next two weeks, sailing with Paul and Skipper Bob, were routine, but exciting, too. Each morning we had a new group of sport fishermen on board. I had never met so many different kinds of grownups in all my life before.

Skipper Bob wasn't too easy to work for. Paul and I, it seemed, never could do anything for him exactly the way he thought it should be done—even such simple things as coiling a rope or sloshing down the deck.

"If you stay aboard long enough," Paul told me, "you get used to him, but who needs it?"

The more I watched Skipper Bob, the more convinced

I was that Dad would make a much better sport-fishing skipper, but I didn't bring up the subject with him again.

Jerry got married without my help, and he and Marilynn went to Lake Tahoe for their honeymoon. His arm was out of its cast, and the Army was breathing down his neck.

Megan had her nineteenth birthday, and right afterward she gave us a surprise. She called Mom from school one afternoon to say she was bringing someone home to supper, and Mom assumed it was another student nurse. The guest, however, turned out to be Dr. Ralph Barrett. He didn't look too much older than Megan. She introduced him and told us he was an intern at the hospital.

Dr. Barrett told us he was twenty-seven, came from a small town up in Nevada, and that when he finished his internship he was going back there to be a general practitioner.

Megan looked flustered all the way from soup to dessert. She usually talks a blue streak at supper. This night she didn't have anything to say except "Please pass the salt."

Mom had put on the best linen tablecloth and napkins when she saw Megan had brought home a man. After everyone finished eating, Dad said, "Well, shall we go into the other room?"

Dr. Barrett had dropped his napkin during supper, so now he had to fish it up from beneath the table. He'd been as quiet as Megan through most of the meal. At Dad's words, he jumped up to help Megan with her chair.

Sometime during supper, though, he had got a corner of the tablecloth tucked inside his belt. Coffee cups, dessert plates, and the sugar bowl crashed to the floor.

Dad's half-empty cup spilled coffee into his lap. Big Dan jumped clear just ahead of the sugar shower. Mom was convulsed with laughter. Big Dan had the same problem. Dad just stared down at the coffee soaking his trousers, and then up at Dr. Barrett.

I thought Megan was going to have an attack of some

kind. "Well, my goodness, Ralph," she managed to say finally, and then she burst out laughing.

Dr. Barrett, surveying the damage, turned brick red. He fished his handkerchief out to mop his face. "Does anyone have a suggestion as to what I should say or do now?"

Big Dan wiped his eyes. "You've just about brought down the house, I'd say, young man. I wouldn't try for an encore, if I were you."

CHAPTER 10

~~~~~~~~~~~~~~~~~~~~~~~~~~~~~~~~

Tishi Goes AWOL

⚓

Mr. Archer went out fishing one more time before I signed off the *Rover* to go back aboard the *Macushla*. "Your father hasn't changed his mind, has he?" he asked me.

"No, sir, I don't think so," I answered.

Mr. Archer frowned. "I've done some checking, and I'm sure he's the man I'd like to put aboard the *Amberjack*. Do you think I could convince him?"

I shook my head. "No, sir. He won't do it."

Skipper Bob wanted me to stay aboard the *Rover*. He'd been paying a dollar an hour, and he offered to raise me fifty cents. I told him I was anxious to get back aboard the *Macushla*—which I was. I wanted to help Dad break in Ken.

Mr. and Mrs. Nakamura came down to the lagoon the first morning Ken sailed with us. They brought Tishi, all bundled up in a blanket. "We're foolish, I know, to see Ken off on so short a voyage." Mrs. Nakamura apologized to Dad. "You will make him be careful?"

"I haven't lost anyone off the *Macushla* yet," Dad assured her, "and I don't intend to."

Before we got out of the slip, Dad invited Mr. Nakamura aboard to see everything there was to be seen about the boat. "She's only a little bucket," Dad told him, "but she's seaworthy, and I've been skippering too long to lose my boat and crew by making a foolish mistake."

Mr. Nakamura grinned. "Ken wouldn't be aboard your boat, Mr. Costello, if we hadn't asked—and found out—that you're considered the best deep-sea skipper sailing from Fisherman's Wharf."

That should have puffed Dad up, and it sure did.

We finally got out into the harbor, with Ken's parents and Tishi waving us off. Dad set course for the Farralones Islands, out beyond the Golden Gate in the steamer lane—the first land sighted by incoming ships. A stiff northwester was chopping the harbor.

"You hang over the stern when you get seasick," I told Ken.

"Who needs to get sick?" Ken's eyes glistened with excitement.

I was the one who got sick that morning—just enough to lose my breakfast.

Off the Farralones, we chummed up a really hungry school. The *Macushla* bucked, pitched, and rolled so much that Dad had to stay with the helm to keep us from swamping. So it was up to Ken and me to haul in the fish.

That was a wild morning. Ken got the knack of jerking

to set the hook, as soon as the fish had the bait. Then he'd brace and flip his catch into the cockpit like an expert.

"Sure you've never done this before?" I asked when we had a breather.

"Japan lives from the sea, Pat. Any Japanese who couldn't catch a few fish would probably starve to death, if he lived across the Pacific. No, I haven't fished before, but I feel as if I've known all about it since I was born. Maybe you can figure it, because I can't."

Dad was delighted with the way Ken caught on to fishing and everything else about the *Macushla*. If I was the jealous type, by the end of that day I would have been pea green—and not from *mal de mer*.

With our limit aboard, Dad started for the Golden Gate. He was so pleased with his crew that he let Ken and me take turns holding the *Macushla* on course. After only a few minutes, Ken had the feel of the boat and was handling her almost like an expert.

We were coming in with the high tide, and freighters and liners were reaching for the Golden Gate, too. It was crystal clear on the water, without a hint of fog. Yet twice Dad had to call to Ken, and once to me, to shear off, because ships were going to pass too close.

"Their bow wave, their following wave—the wake— could easily swamp a boat this size," Dad explained to Ken. I knew this already. "The big ships have the right of way, because we can turn faster and can see them before they ever spot us."

When the *Macushla* was in the slip, with our catch sold at a price that put a happy grin on Dad's face, Ken asked, "How did I do, Mr. Costello? If I'm to stay with you

for the rest of the season, Dad has to hire a full-time dish-
washer."

"Tell your father to start looking for a man," Dad said,
patting Ken's shoulder.

Through the rest of the month of July, Dad, Ken, and I
fished together every day of the week except Sunday. On a
couple of days we got no fish worth mentioning, but most
of the time we had good catches.

Dad should have been content and happy, but he
wasn't. For one thing, the marine insurance rates jumped,
and the *Macushla*'s rate, because of her age, went "out of
sight," as Dad put it.

One evening I was watching TV, Dad was doing his
accounts, and Mom was reading a book. After awhile, Dad
looked up from his desk. "Kate?"

"Yes, Jim?"

"We have a business problem."

"What's that?"

"We're not making any money. With the cost of repairs, the new insurance rates, docking fees, diesel fuel,
tackle, wages, and the nickel-and-dime stuff that adds
up to a lot of dollars when you own a boat, we're lucky just
to break even this month."

Mom laid aside her book. "The price paid for fish by
the wholesalers hasn't risen much, I've noticed. Is it time
to sell the *Macushla* and try something else?"

"Sell the *Macushla?* Nonsense! Fishing is all I know.
What am I going to do?"

"Have you heard from Mr. Archer again?"

Dad shook his head. "Even if I had, it wouldn't change

my earlier decision. Lew Archer might be a good boss, but he'd still be the boss."

"Why don't you talk with Big Dan? He'll be back from his walk in a few minutes."

"I won't talk with him," Dad said, "because he'll ask me, too, if I've heard from Lew Archer again. You know that. Sometimes I think you, Big Dan, and the boys are all on the same side."

Mom picked up her book. "Doesn't it get lonesome over there where you are, Jim?"

Dad turned red. Mom started to read again, quietly turning the pages of her book.

"I think I'll go to bed." It was a sudden decision on my part. "Good night, everybody."

Mom and Dad said good night, and I went upstairs. I was tempted to leave the door of my room open, but I didn't. Even so, I heard the indistinct mumble of their voices for a long time, while I tried to fall asleep. I heard Big Dan come in, tell them good night, and go up to his room.

I drifted off to sleep finally, but my sleep was full of dreams. In one dream, I wanted to stay in school, but Megan said that was silly. Jerry agreed with her. It was a full-dress family council; Big Dan was there, smoking his pipe, and so were Mom and Dad.

Mom agreed with Megan, although I thought she would have been on my side. Big Dan just kept nodding at everything they said. In my dream, I couldn't be sure whose side he was on, but I was afraid to ask. It finally came around to Dad's turn. I was so sure he'd be against

my going to school that I got up to leave the room before
he could speak.

"Wait a minute, Pat," he said in my dream, and it was
Pat he said, not Paddy. "I'm on your side."

I woke up then because Megan had come home from a
date with Dr. Barrett and was calling good night to him
from the front porch. I listened to her heels as she came up
the stairs and went into her room.

I drifted off to sleep again, remembering from my
dream how warm I'd felt when Dad was on my side, with
everyone else trying to talk me down.

The next day was Sunday. Ken and I, for our day off,
planned to take the bus out to the Esplanade. This is along
Pacific Coast Highway, just south of Point Lobos.

There are roller-coaster rides along the Esplanade, as
well as a haunted house and a motorcycle-ride concession
where you can rent light cycles to spin around a safe track.
Frankfurter, hamburger, and cotton-candy stands dot the
Esplanade, too.

With wages to spend, that was for us—but we had to
take Tishi along. The baby-sitter Mrs. Nakamura had
hired when Ken came aboard the *Macushla* had the day
off and was visiting some relatives over in Oakland, across
the bay.

Ken was disappointed to have Tishi along, but she told
me, "Tishi be good all day, Pat. Mama said."

Neither Ken nor I was willing to bet on that promise,
but the little kid surprised us. She kept her word. She
didn't fuss when we took turns doing the roller coaster and

told her it was too rough a ride for her. She even stayed where we told her to, and watched us ride the motorcycles —until we ran out of money.

We sure had run out of money—except for a dime I still had. That meant no bus fare home, and it was an eight or nine mile hike back to Fisherman's Wharf! I could have phoned Dad with the dime, or Ken could have called his father, but we decided against it.

"Why don't we hike it on home through Golden Gate Park?" I suggested. "We'll take turns carrying Tishi if she wears out. We can always telephone when we're closer to home if we have to."

Golden Gate Park runs for nine long blocks south of the Esplanade, but that's only its width. It bites into San Francisco for fifty-two blocks, which is a lot of length. We'd have to walk nearly all of those blocks before we could cut over to Fisherman's Wharf.

The park is full of winding roads, artificial lakes and streams, and forests of trees. Once it was only sand dunes —that is, until a little man came over from London to build the largest and most beautiful artificial park in the world. There is a park in San Francisco named after Mr. John McLaren now, and there's a McLaren Avenue, too. He was a legend, Big Dan says, even before he died.

Mr. McLaren put up a fight whenever it was suggested there be statues in Golden Gate Park. He didn't believe a people's park was the place for statues, and said so—violently. Today there's only one statue in Golden Gate Park, and that's just on the edge, where Ken, Tishi, and I were headed and where we would leave the park to get to Fish-

erman's Wharf. That one statue is of John McLaren himself. It's there because he wouldn't let the city name the
park for him, Big Dan told me. The San Franciscans felt
that this statue was the best way they could remind the
future that Golden Gate Park is really John McLaren's
masterpiece.

Near the John McLaren statue is a replica of the conservatory that's in Kew Gardens, London. Mr. McLaren
built that park, too, before San Francisco adopted him. In
front of the conservatory is a huge clock, made from
flowers and cactus, that really keeps time. We reached
there at four o'clock that afternoon.

Tishi had walked every step of the way. She'd made up
her mind that she was "one of the boys," and got mad
when either of us offered to carry her. She wanted to go
inside the conservatory and see the rare flowers and
plants, so I stretched out on the grass in front of the clock
while Ken took her inside.

It was four-thirty when Ken woke me up. "Where's
Tishi?" He looked worried.

"She was with you."

"She *was*," he admitted, "but I met a guy who went to
school with me in Los Angeles. He's up here on vacation
with his folks. We got to talking, so I sent Tishi out to stay
with you."

"Alone?"

"Of course, alone. Why did you have to go to sleep?"

"You shouldn't have sent her alone. How did I know
you were going to do a stupid thing like that? She could
have gone most anywhere in half an hour!"

"Well, if you'd only stayed awake . . ." Ken stopped and ran his hands across his face, as if to change the worried expression. "What are we fighting about?" he said. "Let's find her."

CHAPTER 11

~~~~~~~~~~~~~~~~~~~~~~~~~~~~~~~~

A Night at Sea

⚓

Tishi wasn't in the conservatory. Behind it is a wooded area about an acre in size. We combed that, but Tishi wasn't there, either, because we called her from one end of it to the other.

Ken and I stood in front of the flower clock again. "I can't go home without her!" He groaned. "No kid can just disappear, or can she?"

I didn't want to answer that question. Instead, I asked, "Do you think we'd better call the police?"

"No." Ken showed a stubborn streak. "If we do that, we admit she's really lost."

"Well, isn't she?"

"We can find her."

We tried—until the clock showed five-thirty. We did the conservatory again, and the wooded area. There were more woods across the road. Traffic was clipping by, but we tried over there, too.

"She never would have got across the boulevard," I told Ken. "And if she'd been hit by a car, there would have been ambulances, as well as police."

"Will you shut up, Pat?" Ken was pale, and a muscle was jumping in his jaw. I could see he was about to panic, and I wasn't far from it. So before both of us fell apart, I made a decision. "I'm going to use our dime to call the police."

"No!" Ken practically screamed.

"Okay, then! I'm going to call Dad or Big Dan, anyway. We need help. They'll know what to do."

Ken sat down on the grass. He leaned his forehead on his knees. "Go ahead," he mumbled.

It took a while to find a telephone booth. Panic was getting closer to me, by that time. I dropped the dime in the slot and dialed.

"Rosso's Meat Market," a cheerful bass voice answered. "Who do you want?"

I'd misdialed. "Please," I begged, "just don't hang up. It's my last dime."

There was a pause. Then the bass voice said, "Who's hanging up? This is a meat market. All we hang up is sides of beef."

"For my last dime, I get a comic!" I muttered.

Someone on the other end of the line had asked the man with a bass voice a question. "It's some kind of a nut," I heard him explain, "but who can tell?"

"A little girl's lost, and I need your help," I told him urgently. "Here's my home number."

"Wait a minute; I'll write it down."

I waited, and then gave him our home number, also

telling him it was listed under James Costello, just in case
I might have mixed up the numbers in my excitement.
"Will you call my Dad or Big Dan?" I asked.

"Is this straight?"

"Yes, sir, it is." My voice cracked. "Please?"

"Okay, kid."

I was never so glad to hear a confident adult voice in
my life! I told him then who I was, and where I was.

Things happened fast in the next fifteen minutes. Two
police cruisers slammed to a stop in front of the conservatory. A few seconds later, Dad, Mom, and Big Dan arrived
in the family car. Mr. and Mrs. Nakamura came next. Dr.
Barrett and Megan drove up in a red MG with Nevada
plates. I remember thinking briefly that he was getting to
be Megan's steady date.

"The neighbors told us where you were," Megan said
to Mom and Dad.

"Would your little girl go off with a stranger?" one officer asked Mrs. Nakamura.

"I don't think so." She was twisting a handkerchief between her hands. "I don't know. If he offered candy . . ."

The police officers spread out and combed the woods
on both sides of the road. They had radioed Tishi's de-
scription to headquarters as soon as they arrived. As they
described her and what she was wearing, it sounded as if
they were talking about a dead person.

Mrs. Nakamura was ready to crack wide open, and
Mom was trying to comfort her. Big Dan was conferring
with the police captain, who'd arrived in a third cruiser to
take charge of the search.

Megan and Dr. Barrett had disappeared into the woods behind the conservatory. The police had already abandoned the search there. "We combed every inch of those woods," one patrolman had told the captain when he arrived.

It was dark now, so no one saw Megan and Dr. Barrett return until they were almost up to the cluster of cruisers, Dad's car, the MG, and the Nakamuras' car.

"Here she is," Megan said. In her arms she had a sleepy Tishi with a tear-streaked face.

The policemen stared at each other, as Mrs. Nakamura grabbed Tishi.

"She was asleep in a stump hole," I heard Megan tell Big Dan. "She had decided to hide from Ken and Pat. But when the police arrived with flashlights, she woke up and got scared, and she wouldn't answer them."

"Why did she answer when *you* called?" he asked, scratching his head.

Megan grinned, and Dr. Barrett put his arm around her waist.

"It was *what* she said that made the difference. Very simple, really."

The police captain got into the conversation. "In the interest of finding other lost kids, what *did* you say, Miss Costello?"

Tishi answered from where she was huddled in Mrs. Nakamura's arms. "She say Tishi not get spanked for being naughty."

"One more question," the captain said. "How did you know she was in *those* woods?"

"It's where I would have gone if I were a little girl."

The captain looked at Big Dan and shrugged. "Your granddaughter?"

"I'm proud to say so."

"It figures." He shrugged again; then asked Megan, "Any chance you might want to join the force?"

"I'll answer that," Dr. Barrett said. "I think not."

Megan nodded in agreement.

Tishi was staring at me with accusing eyes. "Why you go to sleep and lose me, Pat?"

"You and I will talk about that!" Mrs. Nakamura told her firmly.

On Monday, Dad, Ken, and I cruised the *Macushla* up the Marin County coast to the mouth of the Russian River. We had reports the fishing was good there.

We didn't get a bite all day. Fog banked off Point Reyes while we were heading up there, and it was thick and spreading when we finally headed for the Golden Gate at a quarter to five. You couldn't see your hand six inches from the end of your nose! Dad tooled the *Macushla* along at four knots, steering by compass—and instinct.

Then the diesel began to miss, and directly off Point Reyes, it sputtered and stopped completely. Dad couldn't start it again. He got on the radio and reported our position and situation. The fog was all over the vicinity of San Francisco, we learned. Other boats were in worse trouble. The Coast Guard advised Dad to anchor for the night if he could.

Dad could—and so we did. Then he radioed the C.G. to get in touch with Mom and the Nakamuras and tell

them what we were doing. Their talker promised this
would be taken care of.

There was nothing left from our lunches to eat, but we
did have a gallon jug of water aboard.

Condensed fog dripped from our faces as the three of
us huddled in the cockpit. With darkness added to the
dense fog, it was real spooky.

"We'll pick up a tow in the morning," Dad promised
us.

It was getting cold. My stomach growled, and then so
did Ken's. Dad kept blasting with the foghorn. Our only
piece of luck was the glassy, calm sea.

That night was longer than any other I can remember,
until Dad started to talk about himself between blasts on
the foghorn. Kids have a set idea of what their fathers are
like, and they fit everything a father does or says into that
notion. If they're lucky, though, a time comes when they
have to rearrange their minds.

"Big Dan never thought I'd come to any good," Dad
told us, "because I wouldn't follow in his footsteps and become a policeman. There was more to it than that, of
course. I ran away from home to stow away on a ship
when I was your age, Pat. But I picked the wrong ship.
When the skipper found out who I was, he turned back
and put me ashore. Big Dan had helped some of his crew
avoid trouble along the Barbary Coast the night before."

Dad said he'd watched Big Dan work so hard and such
long hours for small pay, always responsible to someone
higher up in the police department, that he decided,
young, to be his own boss if he possibly could.

"With your mother's help, I made it, too, Pat," he said.

"I had to compromise and become a fisherman, with just this boat as my command, but I've always been my own boss."

"How come you didn't finish school beyond the sixth grade?" I asked. "You've only told me that you wished you had."

Dad was quiet for a moment. I thought maybe I'd opened my mouth only to put both of my big feet in it.

"It wasn't Big Dan's fault, or my mother's, either," Dad said finally. "They'd send me off to school, but I found it more interesting along the waterfront. I thought I was too smart to need any more education than I had. They both had to give me up, finally, and let me find a job—cleaning fish."

I tried to imagine Dad sneaking off to stow away on a ship or playing hooky. It wasn't easy.

Dad cleared that up for me. "I haven't always been Mr. Costello, the father of three children and husband to Kate, you know, Paddy. I was a green kid, too, once upon a time, and that doesn't seem to be so long ago tonight."

I didn't know how Ken had taken all this until just before dawn, when he and I stretched out on the cockpit benches, feeling sleepy despite the cold. Dad was forward, checking our anchor cable.

"Pat?" Ken said then.

"What?"

"Pat, you have a great father. I wish mine would break down and talk to me that way sometime."

~~~~~~~~~~~~~~~~~~~~~~~

CHAPTER 12

The Amberjack Lost

⚓

A shrimper, the *Lucky Lady II*, had been stranded in Bodega Bay all night not only by the fog, but because it was stuck on a sandbar. When its skipper, Mr. Pedersen, broke it loose with the morning tide, the Coast Guard talker sent him out to tow us in. The fog lifted as the sun burned down on it, so we made it back to the Fisherman's Wharf lagoon by ten o'clock.

Mr. Hollister sent his engine man up to check our diesel. The fuel line was clogged, and Dad had to pay him twenty dollars for blowing it out.

"If Number One Son had been aboard," Dad said after paying up, "he would have got us in last night."

That went down rough with me, but I didn't say a word.

As Dad was checking the shipping and fishing news in the paper that night, after we both had a nap, he said to me, "Here's an item about your friend, Lew Archer."

"What does it say?"

"He's commissioned Jasper to hire a crew back east, and bring the *Amberjack* out. That's Frank Jasper, the Sausalito skipper who retired last year." Dad scowled. "Old Frank isn't up to that cruise. What's Archer thinking about?"

"What's wrong with Old Frank?"

I'd made a mistake. "*Mr.* Jasper is an elderly man," Dad said, "which is no criticism of him. And he may be Old Frank to me, but he's still *Mr.* Jasper to you, Paddy."

"Yes, sir."

"Jasper doesn't have very good judgment at sea," Dad went on, as if he hadn't called me down. "I've known him for years, and I like him, but judgment at sea is a thing you have or don't have—and that's it."

"Maybe Mr. Archer was desperate. *Somebody* has to bring his boat out to the coast. You turned him down—remember?"

"My memory isn't failing me," Dad said shortly, and then went back to scanning his newspaper.

August was a bad fishing month, and none of the boats sailing from Fisherman's Wharf did well. The *Macushla* took aboard only enough poundage of salmon to pay expenses.

"We keep damming up the northern California rivers to make southern California green," Dad explained, "so it may be that eventually the salmon will stop running altogether."

"What will happen to commercial fishing here then?" I asked. "The only catch we have is salmon."

"There are a few herring," Dad pointed out, "and some shrimp and crabs, but not enough to support the industry."

"What's the solution?"

Dad shrugged wearily. "No one seems to know. They install fish ladders, so salmon can by-pass the dams, but it isn't enough. And they have to have more water in the south to support the population explosion."

"So what's going to happen?"

"Maybe sea water conversion for industrial and agricultural use, but we can't be sure that's a solution, either. I'll tell you one thing I'm afraid of, though."

"What's that?"

"If there is a solution, it may be too late to save commercial salmon fishing up here."

"For Sale" signs, by the end of August, were on the masts of the *Jenny II*, *My Four*, the *Alice*, and *Jordan's Boat*.

The only fishermen doing okay, by the end of August, were the sport-fishing skippers. Their customers were catching only a few salmon apiece, but they kept paying their money to go out.

The commercial-fishing season for salmon ends in the middle of September. The last week in August was too foggy for anyone to go out. Dad was in a desperate mood, and so worried that he had trouble sleeping.

The weather broke on September first. We took the *Macushla* out at three-thirty that morning. Just before we

cast off, Mr. Archer loomed up on the dock above us.
"Keep an eye peeled for my *Amberjack,* will you, Jim?" he
asked.

"She due in today?" Dad said.

"Yep. On the last leg from San Pedro."

"Any trouble aboard?"

"None we know about. I have a bad feeling, though.
It's kept me up all night."

Dad promised we'd "keep an eye peeled", and we
shoved off.

We headed for the Farralones. A fresh wind from the
southwest was clipping froth off the top of heavy swells
out in the open ocean. It was wet aboard, but we were so
glad to be going out again that no one minded.

The salmon were starved and running heavy. We had
our hands full all morning, pulling them aboard.

The wind had been a cool one all morning. It dropped
at noon, while we were breaking to eat lunch, and then
swung into the south. This was a warm wind, fanning the
cold Pacific, and mist began rising all around us.

Dad had the radio set to the emergency band. He and
other skippers always keep it set there when they're not
using it. We weren't paying much attention—there had
been reports of a weekend sailor in trouble because he ran
out of gas and of a cabin cruiser that had collided with a
sailboat down the coast, but no one was hurt.

The mist was now thickening into fog. "We have
enough of a catch," Dad said, "so we'll start in."

He was right about the catch. The *Macushla* was low
in the water from the salmon we'd hauled aboard.

"Mayday!" It was a weak signal, laced with static. "*Amberjack* calling . . ." Static blanked the rest of the message.

Dad was instantly alert.

"Mayday . . ." The signal was weaker, and the static sounded like cats fighting on a back fence.

Dad jumped for the wheelhouse. Somehow, with his ear to the speaker, he sorted the rest of the message out of the interference. The *Amberjack* was in "sinking condition" fifteen miles due west of our present position, with her batteries failing, so there would be no more transmissions.

The Coast Guard talker asked Dad to take the *Macushla* to her. Fog was going to hamper the Coast Guard search, and we were nearest.

"Get our catch over the side," Dad ordered tersely. "Hop to it."

Ken and I did as he said. The *Macushla* lurched full speed ahead into the thickening fog. Dad called back for us to break out the life jackets and put them on. He was shrugging into his own jacket as he spoke.

The *Macushla* ducked into heavy swells, shipping some green water over the bows, as well as spindrift, but Dad's hand stayed heavy on the throttle. Back in the cockpit, Ken and I hung onto anything we could grab.

It took us an hour to cover the fifteen miles to the *Amberjack*'s last radioed position. That was a long, long hour. Knowing that another boat is sinking out there in the murk, or that it may have already sunk with all hands, makes a guy realize that the same thing can happen to him.

Ken must have been having the same thoughts. "A thing like this," he shouted to me over the pounding of the diesel, "makes you wonder, doesn't it?"

"Not about anything pleasant."

"That's for certain!"

We'd reached the *Amberjack*'s position with no sign of her, although visibility was down to twenty feet in the fog.

"Watch for an oil slick or debris on the water," Dad called back to us.

He steered the *Macushla* in widening circles. "Get forward, Paddy, and keep a lookout," he ordered. "You, Ken, watch astern." There was a tone of crisp authority in his voice that I'd never heard before.

Dad will find the Amberjack, *if anyone can,* I thought. *He knows exactly what he's doing.* He had a constant dialogue going with the Coast Guard. The *Amberjack* had been in trouble since last night, but she had only been able to transmit when we heard her Mayday. Earlier, aside from the failing batteries, there had been something else wrong with her radio equipment.

The Coast Guard had picked up this information with their stronger receiving equipment and better static dampeners. The Captain of the Port came on.

"Our air-sea rescue team is up and scouting for them, but the fog is too thick, Jim," he said. "We're rushing a cutter, but she won't be on scene for another two hours. The search is all yours. What's your condition?"

"Seaworthy," was Dad's laconic reply. "Low on fuel, but we'll search until we're out of it. Over and out."

Our circle widened, with the *Macushla* at half-speed

and our foghorn silent so we could hear any sound signal the *Amberjack* might send. I strained my eyes staring into the fog, and listened until my ears ached. I knew Ken was doing the same thing aft.

"Please let us find them," I found myself praying. "Please let us find them in time."

We'd circled for half an hour when I thought I heard a sound. At first I figured it was my imagination. Then I heard it again—the muffled tinkle of a bell. There were no buoys out this far. Now the bell was louder and off our starboard quarter.

"Bell away, five points to starboard," I shouted back to Dad. The bows swung under me, and I grabbed the rail to stay aboard.

"Come take the wheel, Paddy," Dad called.

As soon as I had it, he scrambled forward as lookout. A dark shadow loomed out of the fog. "Astern" Dad yelled, but I'd anticipated him.

The *Macushla's* bows thumped into the *Amberjack* squarely amidships. With the seas running, I backed her off ten feet to keep the boats from battering each other. It would have been an uneven match for the *Macushla!* The *Amberjack* looked like an ocean liner in contrast to the *Macushla's* stubby length.

"Now we're here, what do we do?" Ken asked. He'd joined me in the wheelhouse. "Look at the size of that boat, will you?"

Dad and Captain Jasper were having a conference, shouting back and forth over the noise of the swells.

"What's the trouble?" Dad called.

"Rammed something last night. She's sprung a seam. Engines are flooded out."

"Pumps holding her?"

"So far. All three of my crew are on them below. Where's the Coast Guard?"

"Coming."

"If the seam opens further, we'll sink."

Then we got the bad news, even though we'd turned off our receiver in order to be able to hear any sound of the *Amberjack*. While her *transmitter* was out of commission, she could still receive. "A blow's coming behind this fog, and a good one," was the word from the Coast Guard.

Dad didn't take a second to make up his mind. "We'll transfer some of your diesel fuel to my bucket, and we'll tow you—at least until the cutter picks us up."

Now Dad gave me instructions about some fancy boat handling he wanted me to do. I was to lay the *Macushla* broadside to the *Amberjack*, and keep her at the larger boat's side while Captain Jasper handed down five gallon cans of fuel to Dad. And I was to shear off as soon as Dad grabbed a can, and then lay her in for the next transfer. We began and it worked fine, but the *Macushla* took a terrible battering. Her rail began to splinter, but all Dad said was, "Lay her in again, Paddy."

Next, we had to get a hawser from the *Amberjack* and secure it aft aboard the *Macushla*. Dad let me handle the helm for this operation, too. It was tricky and risky, but we made it.

Dad took over the wheel for the towing. "You're a fine seaman, Paddy!" he said, grinning and slapping my shoulder. "Jerry couldn't have done as well, I'm thinking."

I grinned back. "Will you put that in writing? I want it
for my scrapbook."

"You don't have a scrapbook."

"I'm *going* to have one!"

Dad laughed and eased forward, so as not to snap the
hawser. The diesel labored, the *Macushla* creaked when
the hawser got taut, but then we were towing—at an even
five knots.

Dad patted the wheel. "Come on, Old Girl."

The radio crackled when he snapped on the transmitter. "*Amberjack* in tow," he reported. "All aboard safe.
Where's that cutter?"

The cutter, it seemed, had been dispatched to another
emergency off Bodega Bay. Mr. Archer was sending out a
Red Funnel Line tug to pick up our tow.

"You're smack in the steamer lane there, Costello, so
keep a sharp lookout," was the last Coast Guard transmis-
sion.

~~~~~~~~~~~~~~~~~~~~~~~~~~~~~~~~~~

CHAPTER 13

Disaster

⚓

Dad posted me forward. Ken stayed aft to watch the tow. Dad dug in the tool box and gave him a hand ax.

"Ken, our lives can depend on it," Dad said. "A boat that's towing can't maneuver. If you get my order, cut the *Amberjack* loose—fast. Got it?"

"Yes, sir."

"Paddy?"

"Yes, sir?"

"Keep a lookout as you never have before. Steamers have been warned we're out here. All of them will have a double lookout forward, in any event, because of this fog, and they'll be proceeding slowly, but accidents happen."

"I'll stay alert. I want to get home, too."

"I know you do," Dad said seriously. "My conscience hurts, putting you boys in danger, but I don't know what else I could have done."

"You don't have a landlubber crew aboard," I said, "so

just tell that to your conscience. Ken will agree with me."

After the *Macushla's* rush to find the *Amberjack*, towing her toward the Golden Gate was agonizingly slow. The strain on the engine was terrific, too. The deck shook under my feet when I posted myself in the bows.

Dad didn't spare his boat. He kept her straining ahead as fast as she could tow, trying to cut the risk of our lingering in the steamer lane. It was pitch dark now, with the fog still thick, but a freshening wind was stirring behind us.

All we need is a nice gale! I thought.

Captain Jasper was forward aboard the *Amberjack*, calling to Dad. "The water is rising on us!"

"How fast?" Dad was as calm as if they were passing the time of day.

Captain Jasper sounded slightly panicky. "My boys are wearing out. They can't man the hand pumps much longer."

Dad was silent a moment. "Tell them this," Dad shouted then. "It's a rotten night for a swim! I need both my men aboard here. Tell 'em to pump tonight and rest tomorrow."

"All right, Costello." Captain Jasper ducked below.

I liked the ring of that "I need both my *men* aboard here."

Captain Jasper's next report was that they were now holding their own with the water in the *Amberjack's* hull.

"Good!" Dad said. "Keep it up and we'll all eat breakfast at Fisherman's Wharf."

I'd been hearing ship foghorns blasting all around us

as the night wore on, but none of them dangerously close. The fog thinned as the wind increased. It got harder and harder to keep slack out of the hawser connecting the two boats, but Dad was a master at the helm.

All of a sudden, though, the hawser snapped. The *Macushla*'s sudden surge forward buried her bows and nearly washed me over the side.

"Aboard, Paddy?" Fear edged Dad's voice.

"Yes, sir, still with it."

"Hang on tight." Dad swung her hard to port, coming around to pick up the *Amberjack*'s drifting hawser. "Now —come and get the wheel."

Dad went aft to help Ken fish for the hawser and to make the splice. It was ticklish, but I held the *Macushla* in position despite a rising sea.

Most of the fog had blown off by the time we'd secured our tow again. I eased the *Macushla* forward when Dad gave the signal, thus tightening the tow line.

He came forward and I gave over the wheel.

We'd spent quite some time repairing the break. I'd had to keep watching aft, so I wouldn't back the *Macushla* into the sharp prow of the *Amberjack*, or let that prow crush our stern under water. It took total concentration.

As soon as I was in the bows again, with Dad watching over his shoulder to make sure our tow was secured, I heard the swish of water. I looked to starboard. Bearing directly down on us were steel bows that looked as high as a Nob Hill skyscraper! They were aimed to cross our hawser and would drag both us and the *Amberjack* against them.

"Cut loose!" I yelled.

Dad saw the third ship now. "Hack us free, Ken!"

Ken moved fast. The *Macushla* surged forward again, but I was braced this time. The ship's sides scraped our stern, turning us as she went, and all the power I could get from the boat's diesel wouldn't jerk her out of the suction.

Ken came scrambling forward. Dad fought the wheel. The *Macushla* was turning to dive into the ship's wake, bows on. "Get astern!" Dad yelled.

I glimpsed the ship's churning propeller blades as Ken and I raced for the safety of the stern. Dad burst out of the wheelhouse, stumbled, but then he jumped and reached us—just as the *Macushla*'s bows dipped and her stern rose.

Dad hooked one arm around Ken and his other around me. "Over we go!" he shouted.

And over we went, off the rising stern. Dad kicked, dragging at Ken and me. We flailed at the water with our arms. Then we were buried in pulsing froth and torn away from each other.

My head bobbed up into air just before I thought that my lungs would burst. Gasping, I stared around. I was in white foam as far as I could see. Then Dad's head bobbed up, ten feet from me, and Ken surfaced, too, beyond Dad.

The *Macushla* was gone. All that remained of her was a spreading oil slick. The three of us swam for the *Amberjack*, where four white, scared-looking faces peered down at us. A line hit the water and I grabbed it. One by one, they hauled us on board.

"What happened to the *Macushla*?" I asked Dad.

"The wake put her bows under, she swamped, and then dove for the bottom," he told me. "She broke the suction just enough to keep the three of us out of the ship's propeller. Bless her for that!"

The Red Funnel tug, with Mr. Archer on board, found us at daybreak, riding out heavy seas, but with extra help on the pumps to keep the *Amberjack* afloat.

~~~~~~

CHAPTER 14

Dad, Jerry, and Me

⚓

Dad, Ken, and I were lucky that the propeller of the *Kentish Victory*—that was her name—didn't chop us up into shark bait, and that her wake didn't drown us, but you don't get off scot-free from the kind of ducking we had in the Pacific Ocean. Mom put Dad and me to bed as soon as Mr. Archer drove us home. And that was right after the newspaper reporters had popped flash bulbs at all our faces.

I had a bad cold the next morning and felt too tired to move, but otherwise I was all right. Dad had trouble breathing and was running a fever. Jerry got home from Basic Training the next day on emergency leave. He took Dad to General Hospital. Ken was already there; he had a light case of pneumonia. Dad's case wasn't so light.

For two days he was a really sick man, but then he rallied, and by the first of the following week, he came home. Ken had come home on Thursday of the week before and had been over to see me on Friday. I was still fighting my cold.

Megan just about drove me nuts, making like a nurse. Tishi came over with her mother that first day I was in bed, and I taught Tishi to play checkers. After that, she had her mother or father drop her off every afternoon so we could play checkers. She was really good company, and a sharp little checker player by the end of the week.

Dad, Ken, and I had our pictures in the *San Francisco Chronicle* the day after the *Amberjack* was towed in, and there was a story, too. Mom bought me a scrapbook when I asked her for one. "Fisherman and Two Boys Save Yacht" was the caption over the news story.

Mr. Archer wasn't too happy about his sixty-thousand-dollar sport-fishing boat being called a yacht.

The *Amberjack* was drydocked by Mr. Hollister. She'd run over a derelict of some kind, to judge by the damage to her hull, he said. It was going to take a month to make repairs.

Mr. Archer also came to see me that first day I was in bed with my cold. "From all reports, Jim Costello is a mighty fine seaman," he said. "And, by the way, Jasper tells me that you're a good helmsman. I owe the captain and crew of the *Macushla* a great deal."

"Ken was hanging in there, too," I said. "If he hadn't whacked us loose, two boats would have gone down, probably with all hands."

"I heard about that from Jasper, too," he said. "I'll see Ken at the hospital when I visit your father."

Mr. Archer got up to leave. "By the way, I'm sorry you lost the *Macushla*. Insurance money isn't much compensa-

tion to a man who feels as your father does about his boat.
I wish I knew how I could help."

"It wasn't your fault. We took our chances out there.
No one made us do it."

Mr. Archer started to leave, but then he came back.
"Jasper has quit me to—well, go back into retirement," he
said. "The voyage was too much for him. Do you think
your father might skipper for me now that the *Macushla* is
gone?"

"I don't know, Mr. Archer. I wish he would, but I'm
backing whatever decision he makes—all the way. Dad
knows what he's doing."

By Saturday evening of the week he got home from the
hospital, Dad was up and around. My cold was much better. Jerry and Marilynn came to eat with us. He was catching the midnight bus back to camp. Megan and Dr. Barrett had a dinner date, but he was going to bring her home
right after that.

Big Dan cooked that night because Mom was tired
from spending most of the week looking after Dad at
home. It came out Irish stew, of course.

It was great for all of us to be home again. No one
mentioned the *Macushla* or asked Dad what he was going
to do now. It was after we'd eaten, when all of us had gone
into the living room, that Dad said, "I'd like a conference
with my sons. Shall we take a walk down to the corner?"

"Why not?" Jerry was on his feet. "Excuse me, please,
dear," he said to Marilynn. She nodded.

When the three of us got outside the house, Dad
turned up Bay Street toward Polk. "Should you two be

wondering," he said, "I'm glad the *Macushla* is on the bottom instead of being broken up a few years from now in a shipyard. The marine insurance that I complained about because it cost so much will pay most of her worth."

"She was a great boat," Jerry said.

"Archer came to see me in the hospital. We had a couple of long talks. He offered me salvage rights in the *Amberjack*, but I turned him down."

"Why did you do that?" Jerry asked. "Your claim would be good in any court. You had a line aboard her and she was helpless."

Dad wasn't answering questions tonight. He had something else on his mind. "Archer then wanted me to hire on as his skipper aboard the *Amberjack*, at a better salary than he offered me before. He's a stubborn man, but so am I. I turned that proposition down, too."

I started to ask why, but decided not to. "I guess you still want to be your own boss," I said to Dad, instead. "If that's the way you feel, I'm all for it, and Jerry should be, too."

Jerry gave me a surprised look. "Well, sure, I'm for that, Dad," he said.

"Thanks, fellows." Dad was between us. He took Jerry's arm, and then mine. We'd reached the corner of Bay and Polk, and stopped there under the street light. "When he was through proposing, *I* made a proposition."

Dad faced Jerry and me now. "The insurance money will give me a little operating capital. It won't be enough to buy a better boat than the *Macushla*, or one as good, for commercial fishing. It will be enough to make a decent down payment on the *Amberjack*, however. So I promised to sign over the insurance check to Archer as soon as it comes, and when he heard the rest of my proposition, we were in business."

Neither Jerry nor I said a word. This was all Dad's show. "Do you fellows have the courage of your convictions? Do you still think I can make it as a sport-fishing skipper?"

"Sure, you can," Jerry said. "I've argued with you often enough about that."

"You bet you can," I chimed in.

Dad grinned. "Well, I figure I have *two* Number One Sons. So, for a company name, how about *Jim Costello & Number One Sons?* We'll charter to Archer's company in the off-season for experimental fishing, ranging down off the Mexican coast, perhaps as far south as Peru. That's all arranged. During the salmon season, we'll operate her as a sport-fishing boat from Fisherman's Wharf."

Jerry groaned. "You're forgetting that I'm a GI!"

"That isn't forever," Dad said cheerfully. "In the meantime, your wife will hold up the business end of the enterprise. I've already spoken with her, and she wants to do it. Well, we'd better be getting back now."

My head was spinning as the three of us started back up Bay Street.

"Paddy—Pat, I want you aboard as First Mate at all times when you're not in school," Dad said. "And we want Ken on board, too. We'll pick up a third crewman to handle the *Amberjack.* Oh, by the way, that isn't her name any more."

"What is it?" I asked.

Dad still had his mind on business. "In a few years,

with the Archer charters and the sport-fishing profits, we'll have the boat paid off." Then my question finally registered with Dad.

"Why the *Amberjack* is the *Macushla II* now. What other name could we give her?"